HUNTER

THE HASTINGS SERIES

VANESSA SIENA

HUNTER

Limitless Publishing, LLC
Kailua, HI 96734
www.limitlesspublishing.com

Formatting: Limitless Publishing

ISBN-13: 978-1-64034-801-1

DEDICATION

For Katy, who inspired me to write this book with her love for crime and bad boys.

CHAPTER ONE

Harlow

Going to a community college was never a dream of mine. I've always wanted to go to Yale or Harvard. A good college. An expensive one. But my dreams were crushed when I was just twelve, and my brother, Jagger, packed all of our stuff and moved us to a city no one has ever heard of before. Hastings, Nebraska. The city itself isn't that bad. It's small and has enough stores to keep us alive. I don't even mind all the rain. The sun comes out only about twice a month, but it gives the city a nice, dark but cozy touch. Hastings College isn't the best. Though the teachers give us enough attention and help so we can pass with good grades, the food there is disgusting. Luckily, I have a job waiting tables at a small diner, so I can earn money to buy lunch from the store. I only just started college last summer. Jagger wants me to go. He wants me to get a better life after I graduate. But I doubt I will leave him here all alone. He made some friends here.

Most of them are criminals. Well, at least that's what I think they are. He doesn't talk to me about them very often, but I saw them hang out by the river one night and they didn't really seem nice. They were smoking, which isn't that big of a deal. But the thing that threw me off was the gun lying there next to one of the guys on the broken-down wall. After staring at it, Jagger told me to go home and not wait for him. He's twenty-six, which makes him an adult. I thought dealing with my own business was best for me.

Jagger and I live in a small house. It's a quiet neighborhood. Some of the houses around us are empty. Since we moved here, we didn't see any new people or families come around to even visit them. I've heard people at the diner saying that our neighborhood wasn't safe. But for me it was, and nothing has ever happened before.

We both went through hell, Jagger more than me. Our father was abusive and hit him when he was drunk or came home late from work all pissed and moody. Jagger was only a teen then, but he took all the shit my father gave him. He knew if he hit him back, bad things would happen. Most times I just sat in my room and hoped for better times. Jagger comforted me, telling me that one day he would take me away from that life. He promised to take care of me, always.

Since he kept his promise, I decided to just keep out of his stuff and let him do what he does. Even if I knew he wasn't always being good. He tried to hide his bloody nose multiple times. And a busted lip or black eye doesn't go away overnight. I still

2

didn't try to find out what happened. If he wanted to tell me, he would.

Walking home from the diner I worked at was one of my favorite parts of the day. Plugging in my headphones and listening to good music while walking the long way back to my house was relaxing and my thoughts wouldn't be stuck on studying or work.

I always pass the same stores and houses. I didn't think about getting a car. Not with the little amount of money I earned from work. I don't have my license, but I don't need it right now. Walking is healthy, and if I needed to buy groceries, Jagger would drive me. His car is old. An old pick-up truck he found at a scrapyard. He worked hours on it to make it run again. He did a good job because not once has the truck broken down in ten years.

I was walking down the sidewalk when I realized a car was slowing down next to me. I turned my head to look through the passenger window, recognizing a face I wish wasn't on my mind most of the time. Hunter.

He rolled down the window and let the car come to a stop. He reached over and opened the passenger door from the inside. "Get in."

He was bossy. He came to our house a lot. Jagger and he were very close…almost like brothers. And if it's one guy I could trust other than my brother, it's Hunter. At least, that's what Jagger always told me.

I pulled out my headphones and wrapped them around my phone before pushing it into my bag. Opening the door wider, I climbed in, and before I could even close the door, he drove off. I quickly put my seatbelt on.

"Are you meeting Jagger?" I asked, looking over at him. He had a black hoodie on with the hood over his full head of hair.

"You shouldn't walk home alone when it's dark out." He ignored my question and I rolled my eyes.

"I do it all the time. I'm not a kid anymore, Hunter."

He glared over at me, his normally bright green eyes all dark. "I hate to say this, but your brother really should tell you more about what goes on in the city. It's dangerous. And you're a girl."

I raise an eyebrow at his choice of words and cross my arms. "I can defend myself. I know how to use my hands and feet to hurt people and I also have pepper spray in my bag. But thanks for your concern."

Looks like I shut him up because he just stared straight ahead. He looked angry, though. But that's nothing new. Hunter is always angry. He's either letting out rude things or he just stares at you with emotionless eyes until you feel so uncomfortable that you start wondering if you did something wrong.

I got used to his staring and anger. But most of the times it just throws me off. He's unpredictable and can be an asshole.

The drive to my house was short, and when I opened the door to step out, he did the same. Oh, so he is meeting Jagger.

I took my bag out of the car and closed the door just as Hunter stepped around the car to stand by my side and grab my wrists. I looked down at his hand holding me a bit too tight, then up to his face.

"I don't need you to talk back to me. If I say it's not safe, then I mean it. I'll talk to Jagger." His voice was low and hoarse, and his eyes held mine in place. I nodded. Because I didn't want to make him even more angry or annoyed.

His face relaxed and I think he was surprised by my quick response. He loosened the grip around my wrist and nodded toward the house.

"Go. Jagger will be here soon."

I nodded once again, wondering how this incredibly mysterious guy had such a deep impact in my life and how much I just obeyed him.

I turned and walked up to the door, pulling out my key to unlock it. Before stepping inside, I glanced back at him. He stood there, leaning against his car, pulling out a cigarette and lighting it. All while staring right back at me.

Oh, Hunter. How I wish I could just look right inside your mind the way you look inside of mine.

CHAPTER TWO

Harlow

Sitting on the couch with the TV on and watching Hunter wait for Jagger outside made me think about all the times he came over. They always talked in our small living room. I never actually heard any of what they were talking about because they kept their voices down, and the second I passed them to get to the kitchen, they looked up at me and stopped talking. As soon as I went back to my room, they went on with their conversation.

They keep their secrets, and I hate to admit that I want to know all of what is going on in their lives. It's not like I don't exist. I see their worried expressions and the looks they give me, secretly hoping I won't ask any questions.

Hunter was still standing there, leaning against his car. He's on his third cigarette now. Finally, Jagger arrived and parked his truck behind Hunter's. He got out and walked over to him, holding out his fist to Hunter to give a quick fist

6

bump. Jagger said something to him, looked toward the house, and nodded. Then they started walking up to the front door.

I turned my head back to the television and pulled my knees up to my chest.

The door opened and they walked in. "I'm home, Low," Jagger said, walking up to me and bending down to kiss the top of my head.

I smiled, turning to look up at him. "How was your day?" I asked, knowing he'd worked his ass off again.

"Good. Did you have dinner already? There should be some leftovers in the fridge. Hunter will stay here for the night." Jagger walked over to the kitchen, opening the fridge and taking out two beers.

"He what?" I asked, surprised, looking over at Hunter. He sat down on the armchair, leaning back and taking a beer from Jagger.

"Just for the night. He has a gas leak at his place. And we got some stuff to talk about."

"Oh." I looked over at Hunter, who was taking a sip of his beer. His eyes were trained on me. I got up and walked to the kitchen.

"I'll make dinner." Telling him no was never an option. Never even thought about it. Jagger gave his whole life and time to me. Always. And I said thank you by agreeing with him and obeying.

Standing in front of the fridge, I opened it and looked inside. Some leftover potato salad and spaghetti with meatballs would be our dinner tonight.

As I heated up dinner, Jagger and Hunter weren't

talking. It's almost like they wanted me to know that I have no right to listen to their conversation. They just drank their beers and watched football.

"Low?" I heard Jagger say. I turned my head to look at him and smiled. "Yes?"

"Do you mind starting without me? Something came up," he said and stood up from the couch, shoving his phone into his pocket.

I looked over at Hunter, who was still looking at the TV. Eat dinner alone with him? Oh, boy.

I looked back over to Jagger and nodded. "Sure."

He took three steps, kissed my forehead, and smiled. "Don't worry. I'll be back in an hour." Then he was gone and he left me standing there by the table, not sure about what to say to Hunter.

"Dinner is ready," I finally said. I put the salad into two separate bowls and brought one of them with a full plate of spaghetti over to the living room. I stopped in front of Hunter and held the dishes out for him to take.

"Thanks," was the only thing he said before putting the spaghetti down on the coffee table and starting to eat the salad.

I didn't move for a moment. I just watched him and wondered why I was expecting more from him. More than just a thanks.

"You okay?" he asked, looking up at me with an annoyed expression on his face.

I quickly nodded, turned on my heels, and walked back to the kitchen to grab my food. I sat down on the couch and started eating.

"Is Jagger in trouble?" Not sure why I asked that. Probably because for once I had the chance to make sure he wasn't going to get hurt.

"Not your business." His eyes were on the football game and every muscle in his jaw moved while chewing. Could eating look sexy?

"Well, he's my brother. And I would like to know when he's in trouble or when he could get hurt," I said, hoping he would understand my worries.

"He's doing his job."

Didn't seem like he was up for a conversation. I sighed and leaned back, taking my bowl up to my chin so I wouldn't spill any of the salad on me.

Doing his job. The job I know of is working at the mechanic's, screwing around on some cars and changing the oil and all that. I was hoping someday Jagger would tell me about his other job.

I puckered up my lips and thought of a question I've always wanted to have answered. "Does he take drugs?"

Suddenly, Hunter burst out laughing. I frowned. That was a normal question. Right?

He kept laughing. The wrinkles at the corner of his eyes and the dimple in his left cheek showed me just how funny that question was.

"What?" I asked.

"You're funny. And that's a stupid question." He finally stopped laughing and shook his head at me.

"Well? Yes or no?" God, this guy is something else. One second he's all serious and annoyed, the next he laughs at me like I'm some sort of comedian.

"Of course he does. Who doesn't?"

"Oh."

"Fuck me, you're precious." He was still grinning, but his eyes were back on the tv.

CHAPTER THREE

Harlow

I continued to eat my dinner in silence. After being laughed at, I decided to just stay quiet and not say another word. I got up from the couch and walked back to the kitchen.

"Get me another beer." My jaw clenched and I almost turned around to shoot him an angry glare. I didn't, though. Instead, I opened the fridge and took out a beer. Walking over and handing it to him, I took his empty dishes he held up. I rolled my eyes at his demanding behavior. Even when he wasn't talking he was nagging me.

"You know, I do work at a diner, but I'm not your personal waitress." Maybe telling him off would help.

"That's right, you're not. I don't pay you."

My brows shot up and I almost dropped the dishes. "Excuse me? This is still my house you're sitting in. Why are you being such an asshole?"

"I'm not," he simply said.

11

"Yes, you are. You're being rude to me. I might be younger, but I'm not your puppet!" I stomped back to the kitchen, almost throwing the dishes into the sink. Luckily, they didn't break. But when I turned to snap at him once more, my hand hit the empty glass standing on the edge of the kitchen table and it fell, shattering at my feet.

"Great," I muttered and crouched down to pick up the broken glass.

"You'll hurt yourself." Hunter came down beside me, reaching for my hands to push them away. I pulled back and squeezed the piece of glass in my hand a bit too tightly. I felt a sharp sting and blood started to drip down the palm of my hand.

"Told you. Move."

I stood and stared down at him. "This wouldn't have happened if you'd just let me do it."

"I said move." He nudged my thigh with his elbow, trying to get me away from the glass. "Go put some ice on that."

I finally moved away from him. "We don't have ice."

Letting the water run in the sink, I held my injured hand underneath the cold stream. It wasn't a bad cut and nothing got stuck in the wound. But it still hurt.

My blood was boiling from anger. How could he be so insensitive?

I didn't move. I just watched and waited for the water in the sink to turn from red to white. I heard Hunter picking up the pieces and throwing them in the trashcan.

"Let me see." Suddenly, he was standing right

12

behind me, turning the water off and taking my hand in his. He held it up and looked at it, then took an old kitchen towel sitting next to us on the counter and pressed it against my wound.

"You won't need stitches."

"Oh, good." I sighed. I was annoyed. Why would he even care if I hurt myself? "I can do it myself."

"Where are the Band-Aids?" he asked instead. My brows narrowed.

"I said I can do it myself."

Instead of listening, he took my other hand and pressed it against the towel, gesturing for me to keep pressing down. He started to open all the cabinets, looking for the first aid kit.

"Hunter…" I tried to stop him. "Did you hear me?" But nothing.

I called his name once more, but he still ignored me and opened some more drawers.

"Hunter!" I finally shouted and he froze.

Turning around slowly, I was not expecting him to look at me that way. His eyes were dark and he had a deep fold between his eyebrows. He looked scary as hell.

Suddenly, I didn't feel so confident anymore. I took a step back because I was terrified he was going to do something bad.

He took two steps toward me, not taking his eyes off of me. "Did you just shout at me?"

I swallowed and tried to back up even more. The kitchen counter was preventing me from doing so, though.

"Answer me." He took one last step before he stopped right in front of me. His face was inches away from mine and I could smell his breath. A mix of beer and cigarettes.

"I-I didn't mean to—" I started to say but he cut me off.

He laughed. "Of course you didn't."

I lowered my head, not wanting to look at him anymore. He was scaring me. Not sure if he did it on purpose, but it wasn't a great feeling. His left hand came up, cupping my neck and lifting my head so I made eye contact with him once again.

"I was trying to be nice to you, sweetheart, and then you go and shout at me?" One of his eyebrows rose and my body started to feel all types of tingly. I was nervous. The way his hand was gripping my neck was terrifying. I started to breathe faster, hoping he wouldn't squeeze any harder.

Was he enjoying this? And he sure changed his attitude faster than lightning.

He was probably waiting for me to apologize. But why would I? *He* was being a pain in the ass by not answering or listening to me. So how am *I* the bad guy in this situation? Why was he angry with *me*?

"If you talk to me like that ever again, I will not hesitate. Understood?" I nodded. And now he's threatening me? I wonder what Jagger would say to all of this.

"I'm sorry," I finally said.

He nodded, then let go of me, taking a step back again. "Now, tell me where you keep your first aid kit."

And just like that, all of his anger was gone. He was back to being the emotionless asshole he was before.

But who am I kidding? I like him better emotionless than angry.

CHAPTER FOUR

Harlow

It was almost midnight when Jagger came back home. After Hunter patched up my wounded hand, we sat down on the couch in silence and watched TV. No one said a word. It was awkward. Well, for me it was. Not so sure about Mr. Bipolar over there. I was afraid he would snap from one moment to the next and start shouting at me again.

The way he grabbed me back in the kitchen made me realize that I couldn't trust him. He almost choked me, gripping my neck a little too hard. I knew he wasn't going to hurt me badly. Not when Jagger could get home any second.

I looked over to the front door and let out a relieved breath I was keeping in the whole time. "Are you okay?"

He nodded and locked the door, then walked over to us. "All good," he said, looking over at Hunter. "We'll talk tomorrow."

Hunter nodded once and turned his gaze back to

the TV. My brother smiled at me and ran his hand through my hair once. "Go to bed, yeah? You got work tomorrow."

I nodded. "Good night, Jag."

"Night, Low." With that, he bent down, kissing my head like he always does, and then walked down the small hallway to his room.

My eyes were on Hunter as soon as Jagger closed his door. He wasn't really interested in me. Good. Not that I wanted to get any more shit from him and his personality disorder.

I got up and went to pour myself a glass of water. I thought about just leaving him there and going to my room to sleep. But he didn't have pillows or a blanket for the night.

On one hand, I knew I wasn't rude enough to just not care about him sleeping on the couch and probably freeze at night. On the other, I wished I was stubborn enough to go through with it and not be nice.

I drank the water and put the glass in the sink. Turning, I walked past the couch and into my room. I took one of the two blankets on my bed and grabbed a pillow too. Going back to the living room, I placed them on the empty space next to him. "You'll need this. The heater turns off at midnight. It won't be warm in here until the sun comes up again."

Hunter glanced up at me as if it was the most natural thing that I would bring him a blanket and pillow. "Okay."

I raised an eyebrow and let out a fake laugh. "That's all? Just *okay*? No *thank you, Harlow*? God,

17

you're a dick."

Shaking my head, I turned and stomped to my room. I was probably overreacting. But could he be even more unkind? I should have said no when Jagger said that he would stay here for the night. Why can't I just open my mouth for once and speak my thoughts?

Lying in bed, I stared up at the ceiling, thinking about my not-so-strong attitude. I had to get my shit together and defend myself. I couldn't go on with my life and let people tell me how to act or what to say. Even if it was only Hunter who was making me upset and angry, I didn't want to deal with these feelings. I hated them.

So many thoughts ran through my mind. I was ready to confront him and tell him that he shouldn't treat me that poorly. But I'm probably overanalyzing it all.

Getting more and more tired, I started to drift off and fall asleep entirely.

The next morning I was up early. The diner opened daily at seven, so I had to be there at six to prepare the waffle and pancake mix and wash the fruits for the breakfast rush. I took a quick shower and put on my uniform. It was short, almost not covering up my behind, which made me uncomfortable most of the time when I walked back behind the counter after taking an order or bringing food to the table. I knew people would stare. I've seen them stare at Adeline. She's a college student at Hastings College too. But unlike me, she liked being stared at while working.

I put on my white Converse and walked out of

my bedroom. Knowing Hunter would still be sleeping, I tried to be as quiet as possible. But much to my surprise, as I turned the corner he was sitting on the couch fully clothed.

"You ready?" he asked.

"For what?"

"Work. I'll drive you."

"Huh?"

"You heard me. Come on. I got places to be before your brother wakes up." He got up and walked toward the front door. So he was driving me to work? God, this man is unpredictable.

"You know you don't have to. I can walk. I like walking," I said, not moving my feet.

"Walking the streets of Hastings in that outfit will either get you kidnapped or raped. Or both." His voice was monotonous, as if he didn't even care about what he just said.

"How charming. But I've walked the streets of Hastings for a while now in this outfit and nothing has ever happened."

His eyes shot in my direction and I mentally prepared for an unnecessary comment from him. "Move. Or I swear to God I will take you over my shoulder and walk you out of this damn house."

Oh, my. Bossy much?

I held up my hands in defeat and then walked out the door. Something about him made me curious about his past. What he was like as a kid. What he went through to become like this.

CHAPTER FIVE

Harlow

The drive to the diner was quiet. Hunter didn't say a word. Instead, he lit his cigarette and rolled down the window, holding the steering wheel with his right hand. I wanted to look over at him. I wanted to know if he was angry or annoyed. There wasn't much room for any other emotion, I thought. For what I've seen so far, I only got to know those two sides of him. Either batshit crazy or as calm as the sea. Not sure what scared me more. He's aggressive when he's mad and there were chances to make out his next move. But when he was quiet and didn't show any emotions, God knows what the hell was going on in his mind.

I decided not to look at him. If he would want to talk, then he would, right?

It was only five forty-nine a.m. and he was up, driving me to work. Surely he had something important to do and needed to wake up this early, anyway. But that too, was probably none of my business. Pushing the thoughts aside, I took the hair tie from my wrist and put my hair into a high ponytail. I hated the hairstyle, but Frankie, the owner of the diner, wanted all us waitresses to have our hair tied up like that. He said the customers need to see our pretty faces so they would give us tips. I always thought that was some major bullshit. But hey, what he says goes.

Arriving at the diner, I opened the door and turned to look at Hunter. His eyes were on mine and I couldn't help but smile. He seemed to be thinking about something really hard and couldn't make his mind up.

Well, that's new. "What?" I simply asked. His eyes wandered over my face, my hair, and back to my eyes.

"You're beautiful."

The words not only surprised me, but they seem to amaze Hunter himself. His eyes grew wide for a second, then he turned to look straight ahead. He cleared his throat and turned the key to start the engine. "You'll be late," he said and kept his eyes on the road ahead of him.

My lips pressed into a thin line, keeping me from smiling from ear to ear. Why was him calling me beautiful making me feel so good?

"Thanks for driving. Bye, Hunter." I got out of the car, grabbed my bag, and taking one last look at him, I closed the door and watched him drive off.

Strange man.

Stepping into the diner, I greeted Frankie, who was already washing the fruits and scrambling the eggs. "You okay working the whole day today,

Harlow? Adeline needs to leave after the lunch rush."

I walked behind the counter and into the kitchen, where I now stood next to him. "Oh, of course." I had classes today. But working and earning money were more important at the moment. I had to shop for groceries every week and the paycheck here was just enough that it would be enough to buy food for a week for Jagger and me.

I put on my apron and went over to the big sink to wash my hands.

"I'm sorry I'm late. I was up all night studying for this stupid test I have today. Harlow, did Frankie tell you about me leaving after lunch?" Adeline walked over to the sink and washed her hands too. She's in her last year and will graduate in the summer. I wasn't sure why she wasn't going to a better college. She had money. Her parents owned several stores around town and she was always wearing the most expensive shoes and bags. I never asked why she's even working here. But I didn't want to bother her.

"Yes. He told me." I started to make pancake batter and listened to Adeline talk about her new boyfriend she met at a bar. She wasn't talking to any of us specifically, but we all just listened. The time passed faster that way and I was glad when people were finally starting to come into the diner to get their morning coffee and breakfast.

The diner itself wasn't really big. It has twelve booths and about fifteen stools at the counter for people to sit. Frankie told us that he never renovated. It's all stayed the same since day one and he liked it that way. I liked it too. It was cozy and I felt safe working here.

The day went by quickly and it was almost closing time. On Mondays, the diner closes at nine p.m. Not too late, but most customers were annoyed by it. They wanted to stay and hang out longer and enjoy the time away from their wives.

Walking over to the last man sitting at a booth, I smiled and grabbed his empty glass. "We'll be closing in ten minutes. Here is your check, sir." I put it down in front of him and hoped he would accept the fact that his evening here was coming to an end. The man looked down at the small piece of paper on the table and sighed heavily.

"When will Frankie start to lower the damn prices? It's just fucking Coke. I can get it cheaper at the gas station." He took out his wallet and pulled out a fifty.

"Keep the change. The show you put on here is worth it all, I guess." He looked down at my legs, then traveled up to my skirt before reaching his hand out to touch the back of my thigh.

"Frankie should let people pay to just watch you walk around in this short skirt of yours. I think people would pay good money for that."

I took a step back and grabbed the fifty from his hand. "Thank you, sir. Have a good night." I quickly turned and walked uncomfortably back behind the counter, knowing he would be staring at my behind. I learned to just be polite when men tried to hit on me while I'm working in a short skirt. I was hoping he would leave without saying another word. I watched him as he got up, mumbling something about 'bitches' and 'beer,' then leaving out the front door.

I sighed in relief and walked past the kitchen to Frankie's office. I peeked my head through the door and saw him sitting in his chair, counting the money he made today. "Here. He left fifty." I held the note out to him, but he waved at me. "Keep it. Go home, Harlow."

I smiled and nodded, thanking him, and then leaving out the back door. "Took you long enough, sweetheart."

I jumped, turning my head to the right. Hunter was standing here with a cigarette in his hand and his shoulder leaning up against the wall. He was wearing all black, as always. His hair was messy. Almost as if he were pulling at it all day long.

"You scared me." I crossed my arms. "What are you doing here?" I asked, watching him take a deep pull from his cigarette, then throwing it away while exhaling.

"Picking you up. I told you I don't want you to walk home alone at night."

Perfect. Now I also have a personal bodyguard.

CHAPTER SIX

Harlow

"I'm nineteen, Hunter. I know this city and I know my way back home. I told you this before. Why are you trying to control me?" I knew this would start a fight. But I was stressed out from working all day long and I felt like blowing off some steam. I have seen Hunter mad multiple times since yesterday and he treated me like shit. So, why can't I pick a fight now?

"Don't start," he simply said and gave me a warning look. He headed over to his vehicle.

"Why not? I need a good reason why I should listen to you and get into your car." I crossed my arms and watched him. He turned, raising an eyebrow at my words.

"Get in." He wasn't amused. But neither was I. Well, not really. But I was certainly enjoying this at the moment.

I shook my head and mimicked his facial expression. "No."

It was dark outside but I could see his eyes change in the moonlight. "I said get the fuck in." He was calm, but I knew he was about to explode. Something made me want just that. To see what he was like when he was pushed to the limit. My head was telling me to just move and get into the car. But I couldn't just give up like that. He needed to know he couldn't just boss me around and expect me to do everything he wants me to do.

"And I said no."

His hands balled into fists and the veins in his neck stood out in a matter of seconds. He was trying to hold it together. "Why do you want me to not walk home alone at night?"

His jaw clenched and he was trying so hard not to lose his shit. "I told you before. It's not safe for you." His voice was angry. "Now get in the fucking car...please."

The *please* made me grin. I shook my head. "Not good enough."

"What the hell do you want me to say? What's wrong with me wanting to drive you home because I know something could happen to you, huh?" His voice was louder now. He pointed to the car. "Get in the damn car, Harlow."

I was exaggerating now. He was not having it and I probably wouldn't get far with trying to push him over the edge. After all, he could get violent. Even though I've never seen him punch or hurt anyone, some people at my school were talking about him one day. They said something about an underground fight and him "beating the shit out of Freddy." Poor Freddy. I still wasn't sure if it's true.

I sighed and walked over to the car, passing him on my way. He grabbed my wrist and pulled me back before pushing me against the hood of the car. He put his right hand on the car and the other still held my wrist tightly. His face was right in front of mine and the familiar scent of him mixed with beer and cigarettes rushed up my nose. He smelled good. It should be throwing me off, but it fit him.

"Not sure what you're on about, but you better stop. I'm not gonna take any of your childish bullshit, and if I were you, I would listen to what I say. Have I made myself clear, sweetheart?"

And just like that, I was the scared one again and he had all the power over me. I felt weak. I knew I challenged him by talking back, and I also knew he would get mad. I just nodded, hoping he would loosen his grip on me and step away a few feet.

I had no idea why one minute he made me feel strong and powerful, and scared and unsure the next. He was messing with my head.

"Are you sure you understood what I just said?" he asked and put his right hand on my lower back, right above my ass. "Because it seems like I didn't make myself clear when I told you yesterday."

I wasn't moving. I was staring back at him and it felt like he was looking right into my soul. That made me feel uncomfortable, but I couldn't look away.

This is a mess, I thought.

"What's wrong? Not feeling so confident anymore?" His voice was husky and calmer. But I still caught the amusement in it. His hand traveled up my back, then over my waist and back down to my hip, resting there as he pushed his knee between my legs to push them aside. I leaned back but tried not to fall onto the hood behind me. He was too close and he was making me nervous.

His eyes stayed on mine while he let his hand slip down over my bottom, giving it a squeeze.

"Hunter…" I managed to say before I let out a little noise of surprise. Then I moaned. Just from him touching me the way he did. This man was driving me crazy and I didn't know how to react.

His head bent down and his lips touched the sensitive spot underneath my ear and I couldn't help but suck in a sharp breath. The whole situation was heated and my heart was racing. What was he doing to me?

"Tell me to stop," he said quietly against my skin. I tried to speak but his lips felt too good on my skin. I tilted my head to the side, and when he let go of my hand, I gripped his sweater with one hand and put the other on the side of his neck. I heard him chuckle, and suddenly he moved so that he was standing between my legs, pulling me up so I was sitting on the hood of his car.

His tongue darted out as he licked a line down my neck, leaving a wet trail behind, then kissing the spot right above my collarbone. "Tell me to stop," he repeated. He was probably testing me. Seeing how far I would let him go. The point was, I liked it. The way his hands felt on my body and the way he kissed my neck was incredible. I wanted more.

CHAPTER SEVEN

Harlow

Hunter's hands were all over my body the moment I didn't stop him. His left hand was holding me tight against him, pressing my little body into his hard one. He had some muscles, but it wasn't like he went to the gym. He probably just did some simple workouts at home.

I felt brave, and one of my hands made its way down to his chest. I could feel him tense under my touch and a slight humming sound came out of his mouth, which was close to my ear. He kissed the soft spot beneath it and put one hand on my neck, holding my head in place while he slowly lifted his.

His eyes were on mine, looking a bit confused as to why I wasn't pushing him away from me. The corner of his mouth turned up and he tilted his head to the side, studying me. "You're enjoying this," he said, amused. I was still breathing hard, my chest rising and falling with anticipation, hoping he would put his lips on me again.

29

I didn't say a word. I was scared of saying something that would make him leave me like this, sitting on the hood of his car. His smile grew, but it vanished as quickly as it appeared.

With one hand on my thigh and the other still holding my neck, he let his eyes wander over my body. I could imagine what he was seeing. From where he was standing, he had the perfect view into my neckline, my breasts pushed up by my bra. My legs were spread, and since my uniform was short, I knew it was pushed up all the way to where my legs and hips met. I wasn't sure if my underwear was showing, but it was dark and only the moonlight was shining on us.

I decided not to care what he saw. Watching him eye me intensely made my heart race. And I liked the way he licked his lips as he caressed my thigh up and down. He wasn't speaking, so I thought I wouldn't say a word either and just enjoy the moment.

When he looked back up at me, his eyes were full of desire. For a second I thought he was going to say something, but then decided to not talk and lower his lips to mine. They didn't touch mine, not at first. I could feel his breath against my lips and my body tingled all over again.

What is he doing to me?

My eyes closed and I didn't move. I gripped his sweater with one hand and put my other hand on his arm. I felt him press his hips against my middle, feeling the big bulge. My legs automatically squeezed together so he wouldn't be able to go anywhere. He chuckled and pulled back his head to look at me again.

"I'm not going anywhere, don't worry." He looked amused by my attempt to hold him close. I was surprised by my actions. Especially since I never really got this close to a guy before. Men normally made me nervous. Not because they were oh so charming or flirtatious, but because I knew how cruel some men could get.

Growing up I've learned not to trust anyone but Jagger. He was the only man I respected and loved. The only one who showed me unconditional affection and support in any situation. Our father decided that being a complete asshole would be best while raising two kids on his own. After I was born, Jagger started first grade. He was only seven, but yet managed to feed me and change my diapers every day. Or every time our father wouldn't do it because he was drunk, lying on the couch and watching some stupid show instead of taking care of his son and newborn daughter.

When Jagger started high school, I finally got to go to school too. When Jagger became a freshman in high school, I started first grade. The city we grew up in wasn't big. Therefore, our school had all age groups, from first graders to seniors in our school had all age groups, from kindergarten to high school. I felt safe every time Jagger held my hand, walking me to my classes and glaring at boys who made fun of both of us because of our clothes. I wore Jagger's things up until he started working as a pool boy at fifteen and earned some money. As soon as he had filled his piggy bank, he smashed it and took me to the mall, buying me two full outfits.

It wasn't much, but my heart warms every time I think back to that day. Seeing how happy he was to make me happy was all I needed. He was the best brother anyone could ever imagine, and even now he's doing the best he can to see me smile.

That day at the mall came to a dramatic end. When we got back home with my new clothes, our father was furious. He had been drinking and probably taking some drugs. He freaked out all of a sudden and started to throw things at us. Keys, remotes, even a chair flew. I cried, not knowing what had gotten into him and Jagger tried to calm him down. At seventeen, he wasn't well built. He was slim, didn't eat much because he made sure I had enough. He still managed to push Dad down to the floor, but that didn't end well.

I remember sitting next to Jagger on the floor, crying for help because he wasn't moving. Our father had left after punching Jagger over and over again. I was devastated. I had no phone to call the police or an ambulance, and my crying was so bad that I couldn't do much but sit there next to him, hoping he would wake up again. I fell asleep next to him and the next morning he was on his feet again, telling me it would all be okay.

"Low." I blinked, looking up at a blurry Hunter, who was watching me carefully and frowning. "Are you listening to me?" he asked. He had put some distance between us. I was still sitting on his car and I realized that my eyes were teary.

"What?"

"I said are you listening to me. Jesus, Harlow. What the fuck was that about? You scared me." He

32

put his hand on my cheek, stroking his thumb over my skin underneath my eye. I didn't realize I was sunken that deep into my thoughts. I felt my cheeks heat, and if there would've been any light, Hunter could see how red I was turning.

"I'm sorry." I jumped up and ran my hands through my hair, removing the band holding my ponytail. "I'm sorry," I repeated, turning to him. He was watching me closely.

"I need to go home." Not sure what just happened myself, I hoped he would just agree and take me home. Luckily for me, he didn't ask any more questions and nodded.

I will have to do some explaining to him sooner or later.

Chapter Eight

Harlow

The drive home was silent. Neither of us talked, and I felt a bit ashamed of what Hunter just witnessed right when he was touching and kissing me. I didn't know what came over me. I never had such a realistic and intense memory of my past. I remember dreaming about my father and what he did to Jagger, but after waking up and realizing it was all just a bad dream, I could push the thoughts aside and go on with my day because I knew Jagger and I were doing better now. So much better.

But right now it felt like all the walls I'd built were crumbling down again. I let a guy who treated me like shit just a few hours ago get to me and touch me in a way I didn't think I liked. My head was messing with my heart, and my heart was screaming for help. Deep down I knew Hunter wasn't like my father. Dad had problems, real problems, and he took them all out on his kids. And comparing him to Hunter was not fair. Still, I trusted one guy and one guy only. Jagger.

Again, it wasn't fair when it came to Hunter. I liked the way he touched me. And his lips felt good on my skin. But the things he said to me before were rude. So he was messing with me emotionally and mentally.

The car came to a halt in front of my house. I didn't want to look up at him and I also didn't want to get out of the car. I couldn't without at least thanking him for picking me up after work.

"Wanna tell me about it?" he asked, breaking the awkward silence between us. I shrugged, not knowing if I wanted him to know. Or did Jagger ever tell him about our past? They're friends. They probably talk about some stuff, right?

"You started silently crying while I was touching you. Was I that bad? You could have stopped me, you know." I didn't look at him, but I knew he was smiling. Why didn't I think of that? He probably thought I hated what he was doing and now he feels bad.

I quickly shook my head and turned to look at him. "You did nothing wrong," I assured him.

He nodded, giving me a look saying *so what is it then?*

I sighed, looking back down to my hands. "I really don't want to talk about it."

"You sure? You look like you've seen some sort of monster or something." He pulled out his cigarettes and lit one, pulling deeply to make sure the smoke filled his lungs. He let down the window and propped up his left elbow on the now open frame, holding the cigarette between his middle and pointer finger.

"Yes. I'm sure. I'm sorry. I don't know what came over me," I lied. He nodded again and turned on the engine. I guess that meant for me to get out. I reached down to unbuckle myself, but Hunter's hand touched mine before I could do so.

"Where do you think you're going?" he asked.

I looked up at him, frowning. "Home," I simply said, confused as to why he brought me here, and now wanted me to stay inside his car.

"You need to eat first." He put my hand back into my lap and then the car started to move again.

"Why did you drive home then? What about Jagger?" I asked, still wondering what his plan was.

"Jagger is out anyway." Oh, great. Good that he knows more about where my brother is than I do.

"Why did you drive me home?" I asked again since he smoothly ignored that question.

"Because you were crying a few minutes ago. Then you told me it's nothing, but your eyes tell a whole other story. You seemed terrified. You still do." He took a look at me and shrugged. "You're not okay. And I know girls. When they're sad they won't eat and you have to eat."

Right. "How would you know I wouldn't eat tonight?" I raised a brow, challenging his observation and knowledge of *sad girls*.

He shrugged again. "I wouldn't. But your fridge is empty, anyway."

Looking back down to my hands, I decided to give up right away. He was probably right. It's the end of the month and I had to go grocery shopping soon.

He stayed quiet for a while before stopping at a red light. He took one last pull on his cigarette before throwing it out of the window and rolling it back up. "What do you wanna eat?" he finally asked.

"Ribs and wedges?" I suggested. He looked surprised.

"That was quick," He laughed and puckered his lips. He was amused.

"Why?"

"Because most times girls have a hard time deciding what they want to eat."

There is his knowledge of women again. I rolled my eyes, looking out of the window. "Not every girl is the same, Hunter."

"Yeah, that's right. But you're one of them who stands out the most."

I blushed. How could an arrogant guy like him say words like that and make me feel so special? Yesterday he was all pissed and moody toward me.

"You don't even know me."

"I know enough."

The light turned green and he stepped on the gas, making the car move again.

What did he know? Surely, Jagger never told him about our past and I also never talked to Hunter. Not before he came to sleep over at our place yesterday. So what would he know about me?

"Stop thinking too much, sweetheart."

I realized I was studying my hands intensely, frowning. Looking back up at him, he had his eyes on me but looked back to the road with an almost mischievous smile.

One thing I knew for sure—Hunter read me like a book and I wasn't sure how to feel about it.

CHAPTER NINE

Harlow

We arrived at a diner I knew was open twenty-four/seven. Not sure how they managed to do that, but they were right on the highway where lots of cars drove by, so I guess it makes sense that they never close.

Hunter parked and got out of the car, walking around the front, and just as I thought he would be a gentleman and open my door, he took out his famous cigarettes and lit one. Feeling a bit embarrassed for waiting in the car, thinking he would actually help me out, I finally opened the door and stepped out.

His phone was out in one hand now, and he looked down at the screen, tapping on it now and then. "You can go in. I'll just have to make a quick call," he informed me and took some steps to the side. I nodded, even though he wouldn't see it. He was already holding up his device to his hoodie-covered ear.

I looked up at the sky and the moon was visible for a change. There was usually fog all over Hastings. The sun barely shone and rain was what we got most days. I liked it. Never was a big fan of the big, round burning ball in the sky.

I took one last look over at Hunter, finding him standing there with his eyes on me and lifting one corner of his mouth upwards before I turned to walk into the diner.

It wasn't very different from Frankie's. The booths were newer and the floor was probably newly tiled. It also smelled fresh inside and music was playing from the speakers. A girl behind the counter smiled at me and simply asked: "Dinner?"

I nodded, smiling back at her and deciding that she was polite. Girls at Hastings College were usually in a bad mood most of the times. And more than half of them were obnoxious. I didn't really like them. Mostly because I knew I would never be as fashionable and smart as them. Yes, smart. I wasn't stupid or anything, but those girls were book-smart. I, on the other hand, was street-smart.

That's what Jagger always told me. And still does. He says: "We've been through shit these girls haven't and they would never know what it's like to fight to get somewhere or something. They are spoiled. You, Low, you know what it's like to live. And you know how to survive."

"Will your boyfriend out there come and eat too?" the girl asked me when she stepped around from behind the counter and pointed outside the large window.

"I—" I started to say, looking in the direction she

40

was pointing. "Oh, no. I mean, yes. But he's not my boyfriend."

"Shame." She pouted. I wasn't sure if she was being sarcastic or not, but she showed me to a free table. "Make yourself comfortable. What would you like to drink?"

I sat down, taking off my jacket, then looking at her name which was written on the nameplate.

Bliss.

"That's a nice name," I told her instead of answering her question. She smiled, showing off two very deep dimples in her cheeks. Her red lipstick was perfectly drawn on her lips and it complemented her silver, short hair. Looking at her now, she reminded me of a model.

"Why, thank you, darling. Now, enough about me. Tell me what you and your guy-friend want to drink."

Oh, God. I must be very annoying. "Two Cokes, please."

She went back to the counter, smiling at the other customers in the diner. She sure knew how to be a good waitress.

She was soon back with the two Cokes, putting them down in front of me. "So, you wanna order already, or do you wanna wait for him?" She nodded toward the window and I shook my head.

"We'll have the wedges and ribs, please." She nodded again, grinning this time. "So, are you two on a date or something? Because if you are, I would never wait on a man."

"Oh, no. We're not dating. He's my brother's friend, that's all." I smiled at her, hoping she would finally let that subject go.

"Shame," she said again. "He's handsome." With that, she left the table again and I took a deep breath and leaned back. I just wanted to eat and then go to bed. Is that too much to ask?

About fifteen minutes later, Hunter walked into the diner, walking up to me the second he found me sitting in the booth in the back. He sat down, looking at my face like he was searching for something, then took down his hood to reveal his full head of hair. I liked his hair. It was slightly curled at the ends and the color made his eyes pop even more.

"Did you order already?" he asked. I nodded, pointing to Bliss, who was already coming our way with the food. *That was quick.*

"Ribs and wedges," she said, placing the plates in front of us. "Enjoy. And we do have a good phone connection in here to make a call. You could've at least sat here with her so she wouldn't have been alone."

My mouth opened, surprised by Bliss's comment. I looked over at Hunter, hoping he wouldn't snap at her and get mad just like he did with me when I was being so forward with my thoughts.

Much to my surprise, he grinned. "One reason I shouldn't have come here is because of your unfiltered mouth." They both started laughing and I was confused.

What the hell is going on?

I tried to understand what was happening, and then Bliss said: "Good to see you too, little brother." Then she was gone again.

Little brother?

My eyes traveled from Bliss to Hunter, who had an amused grin on his face. "Surprised?" he asked, taking a sip of his drink.

"Yes," I admitted. "Wait, how old is she? She looks so young."

"Twenty-eight."

"And you are…"

"Twenty-six. Now eat. You gotta get home soon."

Oh. God, I just made a fool out of myself.

CHAPTER TEN

Harlow

We were eating in silence and I couldn't stop watching Hunter. His every move fascinated me and I was trying to find a similarity between him and his sister. They didn't have the same eyes and their noses were also not shaped the same. Hunter's nose was straight. His sister's had a small bump, but it still looked pretty. Hunter's lips were full, whereas Bliss's were slightly thinner.

"Are you done?" he asked, raising an eyebrow and leaning back.

"What?" I looked back up from his lips into his eyes.

"Are you done staring at my lips? Sad that you didn't get a taste of them?" Now he was amused. It always surprised me how fast his mood changed.

"No," I said frowning. "I was just thinking...how come you and Bliss don't look anything alike?"

"You still surprised that I have a sister?" He

grinned, taking a rib and biting into it.

I nodded. "You never talked about her. Never mentioned her."

"Why would I? Not anyone's business who my sister is."

True. "She's nice. I like her."

Hunter just nodded and kept on eating. When both our plates were empty, he got up, pulled out his wallet, and put down some cash. "Let's go. It's late."

I wiped my hands on the tissue and got up too. Bliss walked over to us, smiling at me. "I never got your name, sweetie."

"Oh. I'm Harlow." I smiled back at her, then looked up at Hunter, who was already holding a cigarette between his fingers.

"Come on." God, why was he so pushy all the time?

"You should come here more often, Hun. It's not forbidden to visit a sister at work." Bliss nudged him with her elbow and he rolled his eyes. I smiled at Bliss calling him *Hun*. It just sounded wrong.

"I don't have time to come here every week, Bliss." He looked over at me and nodded toward the exit. "I'm not gonna repeat myself. Go."

I sighed, gave Bliss a small wave, and then walked toward the door. I didn't know why I listened to what he commanded me to do, but I guess I just didn't want to start a fight again. My mind was tired and my body needed some well-deserved sleep.

Walking to his car, I crossed my arms, looking back to the diner where I saw Hunter and Bliss still standing at the booth we just ate. They were arguing about something. Hunter looked annoyed with his sister and Bliss was furiously waving her hands around and pointing at Hunter multiple times.

What could they possibly be arguing about? Me? No. Why would they argue about me? I barely know Hunter, and Bliss I just got to know tonight. Probably some family issues.

Minutes later, Hunter walked out of the diner. "Is everything okay?"

"Get the fuck in," he shouted, his face angry.

Wow. "What the hell are you shouting at me for?" I couldn't help it. I was tired of him taking his bad mood out on me. But as I found out quickly enough, that wasn't a good idea.

Hunter's hand grabbed the back of my head, twisting my hair around his fingers and gripping tightly. My skull hurt instantly and I couldn't help but let out a small cry.

His eyes were burning with sudden rage and the veins on his neck stood out. "How many more times do I have to tell you not to fucking talk back to me? I said to get in the fucking car."

My eyes were tearing up and my heart was racing. I was scared of him, remembering the last time a man hurt me like that. I shut my eyes tightly, hoping for him to let me go.

If someone hurts you, hurt them back. Jagger's voice echoed in my mind, but I couldn't move. The sharp pain coming from the back of my head burned right through my body.

"Please, stop," I croaked out and felt tears run down my cheeks. I was silently begging him to let

46

go, but it wasn't until I heard Bliss's voice breaking this awful silence that Hunter let go of me, taking some steps back and running both of his hands through his hair.

"Damn it, Hunter! She's just a kid." Bliss's arms came around me and I let her hold me. I was shocked by his behavior. "Go home," she then said, stroking my hair. I lifted my head, trying to figure out if she was talking to me or him. "I will take her home. Go, Hunter."

Relieved that she was sending her brother off, I watched Hunter kick the back of his car and then walk over to the driver's seat and get in, muttering curses I didn't quite understand.

As soon as he took off, I hiccupped, letting some more tears stream down my face. "He's difficult. Come on, I'll get you home." I just nodded. I decided not to bother with thoughts of Hunter for now. My head was hurting and I was crying again. I was a mess.

Before Hunter came into my life, I was doing good. I didn't think of the past, about my father, or Jagger fighting for both of us. I was getting better. Happier.

Getting into Bliss's car, I quickly buckled up and took a deep breath. Thoughts of regret ran through me. Why did I ever trust him? Why did I get into his car in the first place, and why did I care so much?

Would I tell Jagger about what he did to me? But then if I did, Hunter had no reason to keep quiet and not tell Jagger about today. Me sitting on the hood of his car while he touched and kissed me. And me liking it was controversial if I would tell Jagger what Hunter did to me just now. I was in deep shit.

"He's not worth crying over, sweetie. He's been this way all of his life. Well, since the first day of living in an orphanage, at least."

CHAPTER ELEVEN

Harlow

Surprised by Bliss's words, I looked over at her. Her hands were on the steering wheel, her knuckles all white from gripping it tightly.

"He was an orphan?" My tears dried on my cheeks and my eyes still slightly burned from crying. Hunter shocked me with his violence. I was trying so hard to understand what I said wrong just before he got so mad at me and pulled my hair so tight I thought it would fall out.

"Yes." She sighed, shaking her head. "But that's not really something I should talk about. It's his story."

"But you're his sister," I pointed out. She laughed.

"Yes, but not biologically." She looked over at me and her expression told me just how much she wished she didn't just tell me that.

"God, I should shut up once in a while," she said under her breath.

49

"So, you two got adopted into the same family?" I asked. I was interested in finding out more about Hunter and his past. Something must have gone terribly wrong in his childhood that made him turn out the way he was today. No man has hate and rage in him from just being…a man, right?

But I could be wrong. I've never learned much about my father to explain why he was such a bad person. What got into his head that made it okay to hit his children. It was all a mystery to me.

"Yes. But that's all I will talk about. You know enough already. And I know Hunter won't appreciate me telling you all of this. So, please…" She looked over at me with a pleading look in her eyes. "Don't tell him you know about him being an orphan, okay? He hates to talk about it and it will get ugly real quick."

I just nodded. Okay, Hunter was an orphan. I could let it go now. And I wasn't so sure he would ever come back to see me after what he did to me. I mean, would he ever have that little empathy to just push the bad things he did to a person aside and act like everything is fine?

We arrived home and I quickly unbuckled before opening the door. "Thank you for driving me, Bliss. And I'm sorry for taking your time." I got out and bent down to look at her again.

"Don't worry, sweetie. Take care, yeah?" And with that, I closed the door and turned around, running off toward the front door and opening it as soon as I reached it.

I couldn't help letting a sob escape. Something in me wanted to get out and I didn't even know I was still holding something in. Feelings came crashing over me like waves and I felt my heart beating loud in my chest.

But the moment I heard footsteps coming from down the hall I held my breath, wanting to calm down instantly and not make a scene.

Jagger walked around the corner, looking all sleepy. He tried to smile but I could tell he was struggling to even keep his eyes open. It was only almost midnight.

"You're back," he said quietly. I nodded, smiling at him and taking off my jacket. "I'm sorry I woke you."

He waved once, letting me know it was okay. "I wasn't asleep, just really tired. Did you eat?" he asked and I nodded again. "Yes. I had something back at the diner. I'm sorry I'm later than usual."

"S'okay. Hunter just texted me that he got you here."

Wait, what?

He yawned and pointed back to his room before turning his back to me. "Go sleep, Low." And with that, he was gone.

Hunter texted *him* that he got me here? Just now? How would Hunter know when I got home when Bliss was the one driving me here?

Confused, I walked over to the living room window and pulled the curtain aside to look outside. It was dark, but not even five seconds later headlights of a car shone through the darkness and I recognized Hunter's car on the other side of the street.

He was here, watching me.

I stood still, wondering if he could see me.

What was he doing? Stalking me after assaulting me? *That guy needs serious help*, I thought.

Waiting for him to drive off, I crossed my arms over my chest, hoping he would see my angry expression. I can't remember how long I stood there, but after some minutes he finally drove off.

What was that all about? First, he treats me like I'm some sort of object he can shout at and then he sits outside my house in his car, guarding me.

I needed to avoid him from now on. What was I even thinking? He was rude to me from the beginning. So why would I even try to let him control me?

Sighing, I walked to my bedroom and took off my uniform. I would use it tomorrow again since I have to take over Adeline's shift.

I was lying in bed and staring at the ceiling. It was almost two a.m., and I couldn't sleep. My thoughts always went back to Hunter the moment I closed my eyes and tried to get some sleep. It was impossible at this point to push him aside. His words and actions last night were too strong for me to just ignore.

I knew I didn't do anything wrong. I was being nice, trying to help him by asking if he was okay. But he snapped and got violent.

Hunter had problems. Big issues. And I wasn't sure I could handle him. Not sure why I even would want to handle him. But something deep down told me to. I was conflicted.

I was starting to mess with my own head. And all thanks to Hunter.

CHAPTER TWELVE

Harlow

The next day went by very fast. I pushed all thoughts of Hunter aside and worked my shift at the diner. Another day missing college. I wasn't sure anymore if I could even keep up with all the courses when I was working so much. I knew my education was very important. I wanted to go places when I graduated, but right now, I wanted to make sure I could help out Jagger with all the bills and food.

Asking Frankie for more money was out of the question. I got enough tips from those weird men. And I didn't want to risk him kicking me out. I liked working at the diner, despite all the comments I got from men triple my age.

It was late already, almost one a.m. and I was tired. I started at nine this morning and had to take over Adeline's shift once again. She said she had to go to an important party. Some guy from college celebrated his birthday at the lake and she couldn't miss it. If I attended classes as much as she did, I might've made some friends too. And I could've gotten invited to that party too.

But here I was, standing behind the counter, waiting for the customers to raise their hands for the check. I expected them to stay longer tonight. It was a rainy night, like most nights, and people found comfort in Frankie's Diner. The music playing lightly in the background and the smell of food in the air made it easy to order one drink after the other and not thinking about going home to sleep.

Not sure people understood how hard it was to walk and stand all day long, talking to people and being polite all the time to try and not piss off any of the paying customers.

"Go home, Harlow." I turned around to see Frankie standing there with a beer in his hand. "I will handle the rest."

"Okay." No need to argue with that. I needed the money, but I knew to tell him that I would wanna work wouldn't get me anywhere.

I made my way home in the rain. I never took an umbrella with me when I left the house. I loved the rain. It made me feel alive and I would take a shower at home, anyway.

Arriving home, I knew Jagger would be asleep. He said he had some things to deal with when I left for work in the morning. He worked at a car repair workshop. He was good at his job since he started out young by fixing his truck. What he did before or after work was none of my business. That's what he and Hunter always told me.

I took a quick shower and got into my pajamas. My bed was waiting for me and I was more than happy to crawl into it. I had to go to college at ten in the morning.

A noise woke me in the middle of the night. I remember feeling annoyed and upset that someone woke me from the peaceful sleep I was having just moments ago. I opened my eyes, looked around my room, and saw a light coming from the hall.

Jagger must be getting some water to drink. But it was taking him way too long. It sounded like he was looking for something, going through all the cabinets in the kitchen and opening the fridge multiple times and closing it with too much force.

I didn't think someone would break into our house. People knew this neighborhood was poor. Not much money was around and if someone was robbing houses in this city, it would be people living here. At least, that's what I heard multiple times from people in the diner and college.

I got up and walked out of my bedroom. Surely, Jagger was just looking for some cigarettes or trying to make a sandwich with the little amount of food we had in our fridge. Looking over to his bedroom door, it was open.

"Jagger?" I asked, walking toward the kitchen only to find Hunter standing there with messy hair and bloodshot eyes. I stood still, carefully watching him. His eyes were on mine and I could tell he was drunk.

"What are you doing here." It wasn't really a question. I suddenly remembered how bad he treated me a night ago. How aggressive and rude he was.

He didn't answer. Instead, he turned around and

kept looking for whatever it was he needed so bad.

I crossed my arms. "Hunter. What are you doing here?" I repeated. "Where is Jagger?"

"Out." Oh, so questions about Jagger he was gladly answering.

"Why are you here?" I stayed calm. He kept on digging around, opening and closing the cabinets and drawers.

"Hunter—"

"So you can forgive me," he interrupted.

Just seconds later I laughed. He couldn't be serious, right? "Excuse me?"

He turned around, his eyes staring into mine and his chest rising and falling faster than usual. "You have to accept my apology."

I narrowed my brows. "What apology? You never said sorry."

"Yes, I did," he insisted.

Was he kidding me? "No, you did not."

"Yes, I did. Now, say you will forgive me."

"You're drunk, Hunter."

He shrugged. "I still mean it."

"Mean *what*? Jesus, Hunter." I put my hand on my forehead, rubbing it. I was going to get a headache from this. He was drunk, not making any sense.

"You're drunk. You need to get some sleep." He shook his head and took a step closer. I stood still. I wasn't scared of him. But I did have some respect. I knew how violent and harsh he could get when he was sober. I didn't want to find out what he was like when he was drunk.

"Let me stay with you." He slurred his words,

56

taking some more steps toward me. I couldn't find words. Why would I let him stay with me? To see how badly he would treat me while drunk?

"You can sleep on the couch."

He almost looked hurt when I said that. "No. I want to sleep in your bed. With you."

My head and heart were pounding. Why did he have to be like this? Why couldn't he just keep his distance instead of always showing up?

My body tensed, and now that he was standing right in front of me, I could smell the alcohol coming from his mouth.

"No."

His hand came up to cup my cheek and I couldn't help but lean into it, closing my eyes for a second.

"I need you to stay close to me tonight. I need to hold you," he whispered, his voice deeper than ever.

I shook my head. "You don't mean that."

"Yes, I do."

I looked up at him and I had a hard time knowing if he was lying or telling the truth.

He figured it out that I was battling my thoughts because a small smile appeared on his lips. "Drunken words are sober thoughts, sweetheart."

CHAPTER THIRTEEN

Harlow

I slowly shook my head, never letting my eyes leave his. He was looking into my soul. At least, that's what it felt like. Why did he have to make it so hard on me? Even when he was drunk, he knew exactly what to do or say to make me feel this way.

I had mixed feelings. I wanted to believe him so bad. I wanted to believe that he meant all he said about wanting me close and needing me. But I also knew that deep down he was still the same Hunter. Not long ago, he shouted at me and hurt me physically. In fact my scalp was still a bit sore from his harsh grip.

My breathing was calm, but inside I was boiling. His hand on my cheek was holding my head in place so I couldn't move to look away.

"When you wake up next to me tomorrow... when you're sober," I said, swallowing and collecting all my courage. "You'll hate yourself for saying all of these things. Or wanting me close."

I felt my eyes water and I wasn't sure why my body felt the need to cry. It was too much.

"You don't know me," he said, letting his eyes wander over my face.

"Yes, I do, Hunter." A sob escaped me and the first tear made its way down my cheek. "I know you enough to know you will treat me like shit once you think straight again. You've done it more than once. And you being drunk just…" I sighed and shook my head.

His thumb caressed my cheek. "Don't cry, sweetheart."

That, for some reason, made me laugh. He couldn't be fucking serious, right?

"How do you expect me not to cry when you fuck with my head like that? I'm tired, Hunter!" I tried to push him away from me, but he pressed into me and now put both of his hands on my head.

"I'm not doing it on purpose." Despite his careless handling of my body, his voice was soft and almost pleading.

"Believe me, sweetheart. I don't mean to hurt you." His eyes were begging. Not sure what for, but he was definitely hoping I would just drop this subject and move on. But how in the world could I just let it all go? He treated me like shit. He was rude to me every time he opened his mouth and his ruthless behavior was messing me up. He might not even realize that but I knew fighting him was senseless.

"That's hard to believe." I stayed calm, surprisingly. I knew he was trouble.

He shook his head and stared back into my eyes.

"Let me show you. Let me show you when I'm sober. I swear I can be different."

I found it all amusing. The moment he opened his eyes in the morning, he would realize where he was, get up, and run off again. Probably throwing some stupid fit before leaving. I wasn't up for that.

"You're drunk." I wanted him to understand that. Even if I had to repeat those words over and over again to get it into his brain, I said them hoping that he would finally give in and let loose so I could go to bed.

"Accept my apology then." And we're back to that. I rolled my eyes, trying to push him off. But I didn't even have to try because his body stood still and didn't move one bit from my attempts to shove him away.

"You never said sorry, Hunter. I think you don't really get the concept of an apology."

Now he grinned. How dare he? God!

"I do. Now you just have to forgive me and everything will be okay again." His tongue touched his bottom lip and his eyes left mine to look at my lips. "Come on, Low. Say it. Say you will forgive me for what I did and said to you."

Oh, so he knew what he did to hurt me. That's one step forward. But this was Hunter I had in front of me.

"I know you like it when I kiss you. And when I touch you," he whispered.

"Hunter…" I was begging now. How was I supposed to take him seriously when he seduced me with his damn words like that?

His mouth came down, close to mine. I felt my

heartbeat speed up and my breath got uneven. "I know you like it. But…I think I have to prove it to you that I'm right, hm?" He was whispering now. How in the world did I get into this situation? I was going strong just a few minutes ago, but every inch he got closer, the more difficult it got for me to think clearly.

I shook my head, but I doubt that it moved even one bit. "Don't," I said, but his lips touched mine and I couldn't stop myself from gripping his sweatshirt tightly with both hands.

Something about his way of getting me to do anything was making me nervous, but also I felt lightheaded all at once. There was something about him I couldn't resist. And I hated myself for that because I knew I would be the one the next morning to feel like shit. Not him.

"I'm sorry," he said into the kiss and put his arms around me. Not sure why, but him saying sorry made me smile. Yet, I wasn't sure he meant it. But for now…it was okay.

His lips parted, letting his tongue dart out and meet mine. His hands were all over my back and once or twice they moved over my ass, gripping it tightly and making me moan. I felt his hardness on my belly, knowing that he was probably already fantasizing too much about what could happen. I couldn't let him get it just like that.

Not when he was drunk.

And not when I was mad at him.

CHAPTER FOURTEEN

Harlow

I knew it wasn't right. Letting him get this close when he was drunk was probably the most stupid thing I could've let happen. In the end, Hunter was still, well...Hunter.

Something about his arms around my waist and his lips moving against mine fought back all the thoughts in my mind, burning with the hope that I would stop him from getting any closer. But I wasn't strong enough to fight back. To push him off me and tell him no.

No wasn't a word he took well. I think that had been made clear multiple times in the last few days. And to be honest, I wasn't going to test that theory out again.

Making out wasn't something I did often. In fact only two other guys have even been this intimate with me in my life. Ben, an exchange student from Europe who was dared to kiss me at a bonfire party, and Will, one of the football players from school. He actually took me on a date but I soon found out he just wanted to get me to have sex with him. That's not really an experience I want to remember.

I pushed the thoughts of those guys aside and concentrated on Hunter. His hands finally settled on my ass, gripping it tightly to keep me from going anywhere. I wasn't, anyway. I liked being held in his arms, his warm body pressing against mine.

My arms made their way up, wrapping around his neck with one hand going through his thick hair. I took a fistful and pulled ever so slightly.

A moan escaped his mouth and I could feel his lips curl up into a small smile. He liked that. Good to know.

Suddenly, he lifted me onto the counter, standing between my legs and pushing himself against me.

My body was on fire and now I realized that every part of my body was sensitive. Mostly the part between my legs, where his length was pressing against me. Even through his jeans and my pajama pants, I could feel his erection.

A groan escaped my mouth in protest the moment he tore his mouth away from mine. I didn't want him to stop, but leaving a trail of kisses down my neck made up for it again. His tongue came out, tasting my skin as he ran his hands down my sides and back up.

My breasts started to ache. Each time his hands slid up my sides, almost touching my breasts, I stopped breathing.

I could easily suffer from heart failure by him flicking his tongue out and running it over parts of my neck and my collarbone.

I knew he was experienced. He probably had it easy with the girls in this town. I knew they fell at his feet the moment he looked at them.

His lips made their way back up to my mouth and I made a pleasing sound he chuckled. God, everything he did made me crazy.

"Sweetheart," he said hoarsely, whispering into the kiss. He was being tender and gentle now and I started to feel like I could trust him. It was strange. My mind was still screaming at me to make him stop and run away, but my heart wanted to stay. It wanted to stay so badly.

Even if he was being gentle now, I tried to form words to tell him to slow down a bit. I needed a minute. But instead, I just pressed into him harder. My body was doing everything my mind didn't want me to do. So much for self-control.

His hand slid back up my side and this time his fingers brushed over the side of my boob, his thumb touching my nipple, which was hard to the touch under the soft fabric of my shirt.

"What do you want, Harlow?" he asked as he kissed the corner of my mouth and then letting his lips brush over the soft spot just underneath my ear. He pulled my earlobe into his mouth, sucking on it and causing me to tremble.

He gave me the chance to tell him to stop. To push him off and go back to bed. Alone. I had the chance to take this moment to remember that this was a bad idea. Letting him this close was already stupid. But I didn't.

I needed his lips to stop teasing me. I couldn't

think straight.

"Tell me, sweetheart. What do you want?"

"Touch me," I whispered, my voice shaking. His hand moved, and the warmth of it was gone, causing me to cry out in frustration. Then I felt him lifting my shirt and I stopped breathing.

The moment my shirt was on the floor, I looked at him, wondering if he liked what he was seeing. I was naked on top. My breasts were right there in front of his face.

"Jesus," he muttered. His hands lifted, cupping each of my breasts. I let out a strangled sound as his eyes swung up to meet mine.

"You're beautiful." He actually looked fascinated.

I smiled, letting my eyes wander off to the living room so I didn't have to return his stare. "You're drunk," I reminded him.

"I mean it. You're beautiful. Your eyes. Your face. Your smile. Your tits." That made me laugh. The choice of his words never failed to make me wonder how he could be so damn blunt without getting smacked across the face. I looked back at him.

He lowered his head, his eyes locked on mine as he pressed a kiss to the top of each breast. Then his hands finally moved, squeezing, and his thumbs pressed against my nipples. I let out a moan to let him know I was enjoying this. Well, my body was. But my mind was still shouting at me for letting him do all that. I decided to ignore my thoughts. Let my body control me for once.

"Fuck, Low," he said right before squeezing my

breasts tighter this time. He pinched each of my nipples, tugging on them. My body was shaking just from him touching my breasts the way only he could and I knew at that moment that I wanted more.

More of his touch.
More of his kisses.
More of Hunter.

CHAPTER FIFTEEN

Harlow

Hunter's eyes stayed on mine the whole time. Wet heat pulled my nipple in and I couldn't help but cry out. His lips were wrapped around my nipple, sucking and licking, while he made sure the other breast got just as much attention.

Grabbing handfuls of Hunter's hair, I couldn't stop myself from pulling at it and keeping him close. I didn't want him to stop. The way he made me feel was incredible and I wasn't sure I wanted to live without it from now on.

"Hunter," I whispered, trying to form a sentence in my mind that made sense. He didn't listen to me calling his name, instead, he lifted his head again, leaving one hand on my breast and putting the other on my neck, tilting my head back and kissing me softly.

I could still taste the alcohol on his tongue and that was the one thing that suddenly bothered me.

"Hunter." This time he said something against

my lips that I didn't quite catch. "We should stop this," I said, finally breaking the kiss. His hands stayed in place, and his eyes were searching my face for answers.

"You don't like it," he said. Not sure if it was a question or not, but it made me smile. How in the world could he think that?

"No, I liked it. But you're drunk. And I'm not sure how you will remember this night when you wake up in the morning." I was a little bit breathless and I was now rethinking my choice of stopping our hot make-out session and his tongue skills.

God, he was messing with my head again.

"I'm not drunk." He puckered his lips and looked down at my breasts, thinking about something. "Maybe I am. But I know I won't regret this in the morning." He was playing with my nipple, pinching and twisting it between his finger and thumb.

"We should go to bed." I wasn't sure just how far we would've gone if I hadn't broken it off. Did he want to have sex? Ha, what a stupid question. Of course he did.

Hunter didn't answer. He was still busy with my nipple and I could tell he was battling his thoughts.

I put my hand on his, stopping it from teasing me. "I let you sleep in my bed." I wasn't sure if that was a good idea. But I didn't like the idea of him sleeping on the couch all alone.

He was a grown man but I could tell something was off. Not the anger issues and the douchy behavior he showed me multiple times. But there was something he was missing in his life. It almost looked like he needed assurance. The second I told him he could sleep in my bed, his eyes lit up and I could see his body relax.

Even after all those things he did and said to me, I knew I had a chance to fix whatever was broken in him. I wasn't selfish. The need to help him was suddenly burning inside of me and I knew I wouldn't be happy with myself if I didn't at least try to find out what was making him have those outbursts of anger and hatred.

Hunter didn't hesitate after realizing what I wanted. Him in my bed with me. He quickly picked up the shirt next to his feet and helped me put it on. I smiled, because from what I've seen in movies or read in books, most of the guys kicked their date out right after sex. Well, we didn't have sex, but it was a sweet gesture.

Taking his hand, he helped me down the counter and pulled me towards my room. I took a glance toward Jagger's room. He still wasn't home.

"Where is Jagger?" I asked, hoping he would tell me.

"Nowhere." Great. Not what I was hoping for. "Don't worry about him, sweetheart."

I sighed, watching as he got into bed, pulling the covers up to his hips. I didn't even realize that he wasn't wearing shoes back in the kitchen. Drunk, but polite enough to take off his shoes at the front door? He was a mystery.

I grabbed my phone off the bedside table and typed a quick message to Jagger. He always said I shouldn't call or text him when he was gone longer than expected. Tonight, I needed him to tell me he was okay.

I simply sent a thumbs-up emoji with a question mark. Not even ten seconds later a thumbs up from his side of the chat came up and I was relieved. I put the phone back down and crawled into bed next to Hunter.

"He's fine," he said, pulling me into his arms and wrapping them around me. This was new to me. Lying in bed with a guy, letting him hold me. It felt strange. And I wasn't sure I should get used to it.

No clue how Hunter would be in the morning. His mood would change and he would be thinking clearer.

That scared me. Knowing he'd be the old Hunter when I wake up. There was no way he changed just like that.

My face was close to his and I looked up at him, smiling when I found him looking back at me. He was studying me and his right hand came up to cup my face. His thumb caressed my cheek and his breath slowly matched mine. Calm and easy.

No shouting.

No hurting.

No fighting.

"What are you thinking about?" he asked in a whisper, not taking his eyes off mine.

"Us." I couldn't lie to him.

His lips curled up into a small smile, then he leaned forward to touch his nose to mine. God, now he's also being adorable?

"We're a mess," he said, closing his eyes and kissing the tip of my nose.

I just nodded. I knew we were. Not sure I was

doing the right thing by letting him sleep here. But as I said before; he probably just needed someone to be there for him. Someone to fix him.

"A beautiful, magnificent mess."

CHAPTER SIXTEEN

Harlow

His words were burning inside of my brain. I couldn't stop looking at him while he slowly fell asleep, his face still close to mine and his arms tightly around me, holding me as if he needed some sort of security.

His hair was messy from me pulling on it before. His lips were slightly parted, but he was breathing through his nose. He looked relaxed. Calm and peaceful. The crease that would appear between his brows was gone and the look of annoyance and anger wasn't to be seen either.

I liked him like this. All serene. And the things he said to me a few minutes ago were rushing through me, leaving a tingling sensation inside of me.

What happened to him? What made him feel like that? All the hate he was carrying inside of him wasn't normal. Maybe he was mistreated at the orphanage. Or the families he was put into weren't good people. Well, anything could've happened.

But I wouldn't push him to tell me. I couldn't. It was his decision and I wouldn't want anyone to tell him about my past either. I'd have to give him time. He opened up to me a bit. Not by telling me about his childhood or anything like that, but he opened up and showed me a different side of him. A softer, sweeter side.

"You're a mystery, Hunter Kane." I reached up to touch his cheek. As my fingers met his skin I felt a warmth come over me. Every time I touched him, a shock, sort of like a lightning strike, ran through my body. It was strange. Never did a person make me feel that way.

Running my fingers slowly through his thick dark locks, I felt his arms tightening around me. A small smile touched my lips and I let him hold me, closing my eyes, wondering what he was dreaming about.

I couldn't sleep, and the moment the front door opened, my eyes did too. Jagger was home. I was still in Hunter's arms, even closer than an hour ago. I knew it was still the middle of the night, and I had to make sure Jagger was okay.

I tried to turn in his arms, loosening his embrace and trying to sit up. "Stay," he mumbled into the pillow. I turned to look at him again, smiling at the sight of him half asleep.

I bent down, kissed his cheek and whispered, "I'll be right back. Jagger's home." With that, I got up. Walking down the narrow hall, I saw Jagger standing at the door with a small duffel bag on his shoulder. He looked at me and gave me a tired smile.

"Hey, sweet girl."

I walked toward him and wrapped my arms around his neck. "I've missed you," I told him, knowing he was only gone for an evening. He chuckled, holding me close with one arm around my back.

"Missed you too."

I wasn't sure if telling him Hunter was lying in my bed was the best idea. I also wasn't sure how he would react to that. He could get mad. Not sure what the positive outturn to that would be. Besides, Hunter's shoes were right there next to the small shoe rack. He would notice them.

I took a step back again, taking a glance at his bag. I knew asking him what's in there would only cause him to shake his head and lift one eyebrow as if to say "none of your business".

I looked back up to his eyes, biting my bottom lip and preparing myself mentally to tell him. "Hunter is here. In my bed. He's sleeping." I stopped, waiting for Jagger's reaction. He didn't answer me. Didn't change his expression. I sighed, trying to think of something to say that wouldn't include alcohol. Telling him Hunter was drunk wasn't a good idea.

"He was already asleep in my bed when I came back from work." Lying to my brother was never my intention. But in this situation, I didn't see any other choice. I also didn't want to give him any more explanations. Maybe that would be enough.

Jagger watched me for a second. He was deciding if I was telling the truth or not, but I could tell he didn't believe me. Yet, he was too tired to discuss any of this with me.

"Send him home in the morning. I'll be asleep." He passed me, carrying his bag with him into his bedroom. As he closed the door, I took a deep breath and walked back to my bedroom. Closing the door behind me, I looked over to the bed. The moonlight was gently shining on his face and I could tell he hadn't moved.

The idea of getting back into bed with him, into his warm embrace, was one I liked. Something about having someone close to me, protecting me, made me want more of it.

I got back into bed, lifting the covers and pulling them up to my chin the second I felt his arms come back around me. I turned to him, looking him in his now open eyes. He was awake.

I smiled, reaching up to grab a fistful of his hair and keeping it there, not pulling, just holding on to it gently.

"I'll remember this night forever."

Our eyes never left each other. I knew he had too much to drink the night before. I knew he said things to me that made me cry, feel hurt. Most of the times I wasn't sure he was taking anything seriously that I said to him. Multiple times I wasn't sure I could trust his words.

But at that moment, the thing he said, I did believe him.

CHAPTER SEVENTEEN

Harlow

I woke up alone in my bed the next morning. Hunter was gone but his scent lingered. Strange how one person's presence could light up a whole room. I immediately felt lonely without his arms wrapped around me, cuddled up together in my blanket. Hunter was gone and the familiar thought of not knowing when I would see him again was back.

He sobered up and woke with me in his arms, and I wondered if he still remembered any of what happened last night. I did, of course. His hands touching my breasts and his lips kissing every inch of them made me feel things I'd never felt. I wasn't really new to boys in general, but I never allowed or even wanted any guy as close as Hunter has been last night.

Leaving my eyes closed for a moment longer, I remembered every second of what he did to me while I sat on the kitchen counter. I wasn't sure I wanted to see Jagger prepare food on that counter ever again, but I knew I wanted to do just what Hunter and I did last night over and over again.

I sighed, pushing the blanket off and sitting up. Stretching and yawning felt so good. As much as I loved being almost crushed by Hunter's strong arms around me at night, I appreciated the space I got right now.

I walked toward the door as I heard Jagger's voice, first from further away and then coming closer.

I opened the door, and just as I was about to step out to the hallway, Jagger came around the corner, passing me but then stopping in his tracks when he realized I was standing there. He turned to look at me, still holding his phone up to his ear.

"Get dressed," he said, then continued down the hall, listening to what the person on the other end of the phone was saying.

I never questioned Jagger or his words. Whatever he did or wanted me to do, I went with it without hesitation.

I showered and got clothed, put my hair in a bun, and left my room to find Jagger sitting on the couch, typing something on his phone. "Where are we going?" I asked, walking to the fridge and taking out a banana.

"If I tell you now, you wouldn't come with me." He got up and pushed his phone into his front pocket and looked at me.

"I think it's clear that we won't talk about Hunter staying in your room last night, right?"

He wasn't mad. But happy wasn't the right word,

either. I guess he was confused. I was too, to be honest. I just nodded, peeling the banana, throwing the peel away, and taking a bite.

"Good girl. Come on." He took his keys and walked out the door. I followed him, closing the door behind me and then getting in his car the second he unlocked it.

"You will probably hate me after today, but this has to be done and I need you with me on this." We started driving and I turned to look at him.

"You're scaring me now, Jag. Where are we going?"

"You'll see when we get there. It won't take long, I promise."

I was starting to get nervous and annoyed. "Jagger," I sighed. "Just tell me, please? I hate not knowing what's coming next."

He laughed, leaning back and relaxing in his seat. "Trust me, sweet girl, I know. And no, that I have no fucking clue what's coming next, either, so you're not alone on that one. I knew this day would come eventually." He puckered his lips, looking straight ahead. "Didn't think it would come so soon though," he almost whispered.

Great. Now he's gone all mysterious on me. Hunter being so secretive was enough, I thought. But I guess my brother decided to torture me too.

"Can you give me a little hint?" I asked, taking the last bite of the banana. Jagger shrugged.

"I don't really want you to jump out of the car if I tell you."

I rolled my eyes at him and shook my head. "I think I would jump out of the car from not handling all this waiting and questioning. Just a hint, Jagger. I already know it's nothing I can be excited about, so why don't you darken my mood a bit more right now and let me prepare myself for whatever is coming?"

He chuckled and kept his eyes on the road. "I'd love to calm you, but I really think you will take some hits at me if you know."

"Jagger," I pleaded, hoping he would stop me from suffering because of his stupid secret. We were on the highway now and it was too late to turn around anyway.

"Please…" I begged, looking over at him. His jaw clenched and his lips were pressed into a thin line.

"All right, all right," he sighed, running one hand through his hair. "Don't hate me for this, okay? We have to do it."

"Just tell me." I was getting impatient now. Did he do something illegal? No. If he did, he wouldn't take me with him, right? God.

"You gotta promise me not to get angry with me. Just stay calm and let me handle the talking when we're there, okay?"

"Jagger, tell me where we're going!" I was demanding now, but I didn't have another choice. I needed to know.

Pressing his lips together once more, his grip tightened on the steering wheel. "We're driving up to Grand Island." He paused for a moment, took a deep breath and then said. "They arrested Dad. Gotta bail him out."

Now, this was far from what I was thinking we

were doing today.

There were two things I wasn't sure of. One, what did he get arrested for, and two, how on earth was he in Nebraska and only thirty minutes away from our home?

Chapter Eighteen

Harlow

I was furious. But I didn't need to start a fight with Jagger because I knew it was gonna be hopeless, and me screaming at him wouldn't get me anywhere.

"Bail him out with what money?" I asked, trying to stay as calm as possible. I felt my face heat up and tears stung my eyes.

Stay strong, Harlow. Don't let that bastard tear you down.

"Don't worry about tha—"

"And why do I need to come with you? It's not like I want to see him," I said, interrupting him. My nerves were starting to shake more and more. I needed to scream at something. Punch something. Maybe I could just go for a punch right in my father's face when I see him.

"You think *I* wanna see him?" He chuckled, but it wasn't a real one. I thought he was about to say more but he stayed quiet after that. Perfect, what now?

I crossed my arms over my chest and leaned back against the seat. Looking straight ahead, I wondered what my father looked like now.

I remember him with a beard and dark hair just like Jagger's. He mostly wore washed-out jeans and a plaid shirt with a white undershirt. He wasn't taking care of himself much. His beard needed trimming and his clothes mostly smelled like alcohol and cigarettes. Not really surprising for a man who spent days after days at bars and strip clubs, leaving his two young children behind at home, taking care of themselves.

I couldn't remember the last time I called him dad. Calling him by his name wasn't an option either. So I referred to him simply as *him* or *my father*. But even that didn't feel right. A father was supposed to care. A father was supposed to protect their children from evil, not be evil to them himself.

Understanding that just alcohol made him do what he did was not easy. Alcohol's a drug that takes control over your brain and you don't even realize it. It was normal for some to get angry while drunk. It's a side effect. It could also make people emotional…Hunter, for example.

But this wasn't about the guy who messed with my head and feelings. This was about the guy who ruined my childhood, who messed up any idea of a family I ever had, but who thankfully made me realize that I had at least one person who loved me.

I looked over at Jagger, reaching out to touch his shoulder. "I love you," I said. He looked over at me, the same fear and sadness lingering in his eyes.

"I love you too." He put his left hand on mine, squeezing it and looking back to the road. "I'm sorry I'm dragging you into this, but I need you with me."

I slowly nodded. "Okay."

We arrived in Grand Island and I was amazed how much of a difference thirty minutes made for the weather. The sun was shining and everything looked dried up. This town was the opposite of Hastings and I had to admit that I missed the rain already.

Jagger parked outside the police department. He turned to me and studied my face before he started talking. "Let me do the talking. I know this sounds stupid and not necessary…" He stopped, looking down at his hands. "But I really just want to tell him how much better we're doing without him."

I was surprised to hear that. "So you wanted to come here to make him feel bad about himself?"

"I know it's stupid, but—"

"Stupid? God, Jagger. Why didn't you tell me before?" I laughed and shook my head. "But I guess bailing him out is the bad thing about all this."

Jagger smiled and nodded. "See it as a way of saying goodbye to him forever. Paying our last respects to him. Then we'll go home and we'll never talk about him again."

I knew what Jagger meant by that. He wanted to close this chapter in his life and move on. But I guess he didn't think it through.

"He came to Grand Island and got arrested. His home is in Nevada, Jagger. We're in Nebraska.

That's a long way. Don't you think he came here for a reason?"

Jagger shrugged. "I don't care what he wants. I'll tell him to fuck off."

He was so sure that would be enough to keep him away. I was hoping it would be enough. But I had a bad feeling about it all.

"Come on. It'll be fine, Low."

I had to step back now and let Jagger handle it all. Maybe if he saw what Jagger was like now he'd get scared and never come close to us ever again. I was positive that our father wasn't going to recognize us. Jagger changed a lot. He worked out and his face grew just as much as his adultness.

I wasn't going to ruin this day, because my father would do that for me anyway. But I had to let Jagger go through with his plan.

The outcome of this being positive or not, he needed this.

CHAPTER NINETEEN

Harlow

I walked into the police department holding Jagger's hand tightly. He squeezed mine gently, silently telling me that it would be okay. That he was here with me and that nothing could ever harm me.

Jagger was determined to speak his mind as soon as he was standing in front of our father. He knew exactly what he wanted to say to him and I wasn't going to stop him. The closer we got to him, the more my stomach twisted into knots.

"We're here to see Dean Curtis," Jagger said to the officer standing behind the front desk. He looked up at us, giving us an all-over look and nodding.

He pointed to a glass door. "Walk through there. Security will do a body check, then you'll get some paperwork to fill out."

Jagger nodded once, looking at me and taking a deep breath. "Come on." He pulled me toward the door to a sitting area and a body check station, sort of like the ones you'd find at an airport.

Another officer walked over to us, nodding toward our jackets and indicating to take them off. We quickly did, putting them on the small table next to us. "Go through one by one. My colleague will do a quick body check after."

Jagger went first, letting the officer on the other side check his body for guns. That's when I held my breath. Jagger has had guns on him most of his life. At least since we moved to Hastings. I knew about the guns he carried with him. For protection, of course.

I watched him closely, but he just grinned at me like a little mischievous boy. He knew exactly what I was thinking and I just shook my head, sighing in relief.

"Next," the officer said, and I quickly walked through the body scanner. I was checked too, but not as thoroughly as Jagger. I guess I look innocent enough.

"Fill this out. Don't leave out anything, and sign on every page. When you're finished, you will bring it over to my other colleague and he'll look it over." The officer gave us a clipboard with some documents on it.

"Yes, sir," Jagger answered politely, and we took a seat in the sitting area.

"Let's see…" He studied the first paper, clicking the end of the pen multiple times before he started writing our names and address.

"Dean won't see this, right? I don't want him to know where we live."

He chuckled, looking at me with an amused grin. "*Dean?*"

I shrugged. "After this, he will be a stranger to us."

"Yeah, I guess. Just sounds weird hearing you say his name." He continued writing all the information and I leaned back, crossing my arms over my chest. I suddenly had chills running over my body.

I reminded myself not to freak out. It wouldn't help if I wanted Dean to know that he's no longer part of my life. I needed him to know that I was nonchalant to this situation. That I came for Jagger. Not for his sake. I needed him to see what we grew up to be. Jagger and I. We made it this far without him and he was the big bump in the road at the beginning of our lives.

He didn't do any good in his time as a father. He just left us with unforgivable memories and scars. For Jagger even literal scars.

I looked over at him. He was concentrated on writing. I let my eyes wander down to his jaw until I saw the white line starting just below his ear and ending in the middle of the side of his neck. Dean thought it was a good idea to attack his nine-year-old son with a kitchen knife. Luckily, he was sane enough to call the ambulance before Jagger bled out. He ran after calling help, of course. What a hero. A role model even.

I rolled my eyes at my sarcasm and sighed, touching my hand to his left forearm. "I'll be done in just a minute, sweet girl," he assured me. He felt my nervousness and I felt his determination.

"Want me to get some water?" I asked, thinking it would be a great idea to get some cold liquid into our bodies before getting all heated up in front of Dean.

"Yeah." I got up and walked over to the water dispenser and got two cups of ice water. As I turned to walk back to Jagger, the glass doors opened and a man in black jeans and a black tight turtleneck sweater, about Jagger's age, walked into the room, going straight to one of the officers.

He whispered something to him in a low voice and I was suddenly all ears when I heard Dean's name fall from his lips. Jagger also looked up, raising his eyebrows and waiting for the officer to respond to the man. He nodded once, jerking his head toward Jagger and me. I sat back down next to my brother, who was watching them closely.

The man walked over to us, looking at me first, and then meeting Jagger's eyes. "You're here for Dean Curtis? How are you related to him?"

"He's our father," Jagger said, now leaning back and letting the man take the clipboard from him.

The guy nodded slowly, taking another look at me and then down at the paper. He read the top part, nodded slowly and said, "I'm Tripp Bennett. Police detective. Seems like I've got to take you two to my office."

CHAPTER TWENTY

Harlow

Jagger and I exchanged confused looks. Why would a police detective want to talk to us? We came here to bail out Dean, not to be questioned.

"I'm sorry, Mr. Bennett. But what's the reason for that?" Jagger asked, shoving his fists into his pockets. The guy probably didn't realize it, but Jag was pissed. Annoyed by the fact he couldn't just go up to Dean and say whatever he was planning on saying to his face.

"Dean Curtis told us about the things that happened in the past. I need you two to testify. See if what he told me matches your story."

Now, this is going to be fun. Jagger and I both shook our heads, knowing exactly that whatever Dean told him was wrong. So Jagger nodded und shrugged, knowing we weren't the bad guys here.

We were taken to an office in the far back of the police station. The lights were dimmed, and Mr. Bennett nodded to a brown couch, indicating us to

89

take a seat.

"Water?" he asked, walking over to what looked like a little bar with different types of beverages on it. He opened the mini fridge underneath it and pulled out a bottle of water.

"No, thank you," Jag and I said simultaneously. Bennett poured himself a glass, then walked over to the couch in front of us and sat down.

"All right," he said, first taking a sip of water, then taking out a small binder out of underneath the coffee table. "First, I would like you both to state your name and birthdate." Before Jagger started to say anything, Bennett opened the binder and pulled out a piece of paper, which looked like our birth certificates were copied on.

Really? Wow, today's really gonna get interesting.

"Name's Jagger Dean Curtis." I cringed, remembering his middle name was the same as my father's. "Born February 17th, 1993." Bennett nodded, checking what was written on the copy. He then looked up at me.

"Uh, Harlow Ann Curtis." Saying my middle name made me feel sick as well. It was my mother's first name. Not sure why they decided to name their children after themselves. Seems unnecessary if you go on and mess up your kids' lives anyway. "I was born on October 1st, 1999."

Bennet nodded as if agreeing with me, then put the paper down and grabbed his notebook and a pen. "Now, I want you two to explain to me what your childhood was like. Starting with you, Jagger. Don't leave out any details. Be blunt with your words. I need to know everything."

Jagger sighed and leaned back. I looked at him, knowing whatever he would say would bring me to tears. I was hoping it wouldn't. I couldn't start crying in front of a stranger. Last time I cried was in front of Hunter. The timing wasn't really good either, and I still owed him an explanation. Well, he didn't ask for one that night. So he probably didn't care much about it. I don't blame him.

"I remember the things he did from when I was about four and on," Jagger started, reaching out to grab my hand. I let him hold my right hand, and with my left hand, I covered his hand, gripping it tightly.

Listening to what Jagger was saying was hard. I knew I'd have to face it all one day. Or at least be able to look past all that and never think back. I was hoping whatever Jagger was telling Bennett was enough so I wouldn't have to tell him my point of view. I hated talking about it. And just listening to Jag and how he told the story of how badly our father treated us was messing with my head. I wanted to go home. Leave the money for Dean and then get out of here and drive back to Hastings.

At some point, I closed my eyes. I was holding back so many things. Jagger was very explicit with his story. He didn't leave out much, but when he did, I had to try very hard not to interrupt him and add some parts he missed out.

I looked at Bennett. He was taking notes and comparing some things to another piece of paper in front of him.

"That's pretty much all I remember."

Bennett nodded once, looking over at me and then back at Jagger. "I think I got enough. Thank you."

I let out a relieved sigh and Jagger squeezed my hand. "We'll be home soon," he assured me with a tight smile. I just nodded.

"I'll let you two calm down before I let you see him." He stood up, took his binder and stepped out of the office, leaving Jag and me sitting there in silence.

Neither of us said anything. Jagger pulled me closer, putting his arms around me tightly and kissing the top of my head. He was comforting me because he knew how much it all bothered me. The past was hell for both of us and I wanted to be there for him just as much as he's there for me.

"You're strong, smart, and beautiful. I can't wait to see his face the second he sees how incredible his daughter grew up to be and all that without him. We made it this far without him. I'm here. You know that." I nodded, letting my tears hit his shirt.

"No matter what will be after today, what's important is that we're together. And you know I will never let you get hurt."

I knew. Because all of these years with him I was healthy. I never had any problems, never got hurt by anything or anyone. All thanks to my big brother who supported and watched me.

How in the world did I get so lucky?

"I'm here for you too," I said, hugging him tighter.

"I know. Never doubted that, sweet girl."

CHAPTER TWENTY-ONE

Harlow

"Ready?" Bennett asked us both, standing in front of the door that would lead us to our father.

Jagger squeezed my hand tightly, nodding once, and then looking at me with a small smile. "We'll survive this," he said jokingly. I gave a tight smile back, wondering how he wasn't shaking like I was. My insides were twisting and turning and my head was filled with thought, rushing and swirling around in my mind and making me lightheaded.

"In you go." Bennett opened the door and for a second I closed my eyes tightly, wanting to remember the way Dean looked like the last time I saw him.

His eyes matched Jagger's and his hair was falling down the side of his face in big waves. Some of it covered his eyes most of the time, making his eyes look darker than they actually were. The dark circles under his eyes made him look tired, but I always wondered how he could be tired by sleeping

93

all day long after a night of drinking. The wrinkles by his eyes weren't deep, but they hinted that he wasn't very young. His lips were thin and almost white. His blood wasn't happy with all the alcohol traveling through his body. His full beard covered his jaw and neck. The clothes he wore made him look like some sort of craftsman, but instead of fixing things, he broke them.

"Look at you..." That deep, growling voice cut through me like a sharp knife and I looked up, seeing the man I despised the most sitting in front of me. Other than white hair peeking through his full locks, he hadn't changed. At all.

I felt Jagger's hand tighten on mine even more and I heard him take in a deep breath. It was impossible for him not to feel any type of fear or nervousness while standing in front of Dean. He was trying to stay strong for me. To make sure I felt protected at all times. But he realized quickly that he wouldn't be able to keep it together enough not to seem weak.

I didn't blame him. We'd not seen Dean in years. And now we were standing in front of him, not moving and waiting for him to say more.

"Aren't you going to say hello to your father?" Dean said, looking at Jagger first, then shifting his eyes in my direction. He was sitting at a large table, his elbows leaning on it and his wrists handcuffed to a small metal handle fixed onto the table.

I still couldn't talk. It felt like someone ripped out my vocal cords and cut out my tongue. "Am I scaring you, angel face?" That made my stomach turn and almost empty itself.

"Don't call her that." Jagger took a step forward and pulled me behind him.

Dean looked up at Jagger again, raising a brow in surprise. "Is she not able to talk on her own?" he mocked. A small smirk appeared on his face and I was close to kicking him in the nuts. God, what a dick.

"She simply chooses not to talk to you." Jag took another deep breath, still holding my hand firmly in his and stroking my fingers with his thumb to calm me down.

"I was hoping not to see you ever again. But here we are. Fucked up once more and I'm the one digging you out of this shit."

"I didn't do shit, son. Not my fault people get so damn annoyed when I want some drinks." Dean looked at Bennett. "Getting arrested for buying drinks at bars is fucking stupid."

"You were arrested for drunk driving, Curtis. Now, no more swearing," Bennett said, nodding toward me to indicate that I was standing right there, hearing every word they were saying. I didn't mind swearing. Not at all. Hell, I swore sometimes. But we were at a police station, surrounded by cops who probably were gonna make him shut up in another way if he kept using such words.

"So you're still a big fat liar," Jagger said in an almost laugh. He shook his head, looking down and rubbing his eyes. "There is so much I wanna throw at your face right now…" He looked back up. "But you'll probably take my words and twist them the way you like it. We'll pay to bail you out, but you will go back to where you came from. We don't need you around."

As if he didn't just hear what Jagger said, Dean looked back at me and smiled this time. It looked almost real. I had to remind myself that this man was no good. Never has been.

"Has your brother been treating you badly that you're not speaking up for yourself, angel face?"

I felt my heartbeat quicken and my hands got cold and tingly. A feeling of sickness came over me once again and I was ready to shout.

"I said not to fucking call her like that!" Jagger warned, and Bennett suddenly stepped between the three of us. "All right, that's enough. Step outside," he demanded.

"Don't come any closer to us from here on." Jagger was threatening him now and I was happy he dragged me out of that room.

"Are you okay?" I asked quietly, following him with quick steps to the front desk. He didn't answer me, instead, he pulled out his wallet and took out his card.

"Make it quick," Jagger said to the officer sitting at the desk. He pointed to the card reader and typed something into the computer. "That would be five thousand dollars for Mr. Dean Curtis' bail. Please put the card in and accept the payment. Sign on the monitor after."

Five thousand dollars?

While Jagger was doing what the cop said, I tried to wrap my head around how much money he just paid for this.

"We'll keep in touch, all right?" I turned to see Bennet walking toward us.

Jagger just nodded. "Thank you. Have a great one." He pulled me out of the police station, dragging me over to his car and opening the passenger door for me.

"Get in." He was furious. Not because of me, but because of Dean. I understood that and wasn't going to take this personally.

I simply got into the car and buckled up, waiting for Jagger to get inside too. As soon as he was sitting next to me he started the engine and drove off.

I planned on asking him about the money. How he got that amount and why he could afford that. But not right now.

He needed to calm down first.

Just as I looked down to my lap, my phone vibrated and I took it out of my jacket, reading what was written on my screen.

Hunter: Text me when you're back.

CHAPTER TWENTY-TWO

Hunter

Leaving her alone in her bed that morning was hard. Never thought I would feel empty the second I didn't hold her in my arms. I felt my body turn cold, standing in her doorway and watching her sleep peacefully for a minute.

She was beautiful. Inside and out. I even told her she's beautiful once…or multiple times. I didn't remember. But each time I complimented her, her cheeks turned bright red and she immediately shook her head to tell me I should stop saying it. How could I, though? I never felt the urge to call a woman pretty. Never in my life have I had the will to compliment a girl.

I never even had to try catching someone's attention because the attraction was always mutual. They saw me, came up to me, and asked if I was up for some fun. I always was. Girls were easy in this city. They weren't very talkative and liked to head straight to bed without hesitation.

I liked them easy. I liked them willing and wild. I liked the way they didn't even need to know my name or where I came from to let me fuck them.

But Harlow? Oh, sweet Harlow…

There were certain moments in my life I questioned my being. Why was I here? Why on earth did I deserve to live on this planet?

I wasn't a good man. I had hatred in me. I wasn't sure where it came from and it sure as hell bothered the fuck out of me. I had a shit past. But then, most people did and they didn't go around hurting people or messing with their heads. That's exactly what I was doing to Harlow.

That innocent, kind-hearted girl crashed into my mind in one big bang and I hated myself for letting her close.

I hated myself for letting her see the evil I was. The hate and my abusiveness toward her was nothing she deserved. Her past was fucked up too, just like mine and Jagger's.

Jagger, my best friend who I trusted most in this life, had no fucking idea how wrong and twisted I treated his little sister. His beloved sister he had to protect from a violent and sick father at a young age.

Go figure, I was now treating her just the same.

I wasn't sure Harlow knew Jagger told me about their past. That night I picked her up from the diner and got close to her, so damn close I thought I got addicted to her, that night she had the breakdown right in front of me and I acted like I didn't know why.

I was an idiot. I should've held her. Calmed her

down and told her she's safe with me. But in her mind, she probably wasn't. I was touching her places she's only been touched by that bastard she had as a father.

The thing was, I didn't want her to get attached. I tried to find the balance between too close and too far, but it seemed like I couldn't get close enough to her.

Fuck.

Last night I put on quite a show. Drunk and angry at myself, I showed up to her house, knowing she was alone because Jagger had to handle some things. I knew she was alone and I wanted to protect her from the outside world. From strangers who could've walked into that house of hers and do things to her.

The funny thing is, I was probably the one she needed protection from.

I was making noise in the kitchen on purpose. I wanted her to wake up and I wanted her to see me. Drunk. How fucking stupid was I?

The second she stepped into the hallway in her cute pajamas I almost lost it. Hearing her say my name made my body turn warm again. The cold feeling was gone instantly and all my worries disappeared. I needed her. I needed her more than I realized.

I knew it was wrong touching and kissing her while drunk. But just like that damn alcohol, I was addicted to her. I tried my best not to move quickly. Not to scare her off or make her hate me.

But then, I wasn't sure she was even capable of hating someone. All the things I did to her in that short time were horrible. I was an asshole. I fucked up. Yet she was there, letting me suck on her perfect breasts and make her moan my name on the damn kitchen counter.

Fuck.

I was feeling dizzy while I made her feel good under my touch. She wanted it. I knew she did. She enjoyed the things I did to her and I loved the way she surrendered herself to me. Once again.

She knew when to stop, though. She knew her limits. And hell, I was ready to step over those limits with her. When she was ready, that is.

In bed, cuddled up with her, I told her we were a mess. A magnificent mess. It was stupid. But true.

There wasn't much more I remembered from last night.

All I knew was I shouldn't have left. I wanted to keep her tucked by my side under the covers and feel her heartbeat against mine.

Hunter: *Text me when you're back*.

I sent an hour ago.

Jagger told me where they went. He also knew I've spent the night in his sister's bed. His fist hitting my nose this morning was needed. I owed him. But he also told me not to mess with her and to leave her alone.

I couldn't. I needed to see her.

Harlow: *Meet me behind the diner.*

Chapter Twenty-Three

Harlow

After a quick change into my work clothes, Jagger gave me a lift to the diner. He said he needed to go check on something and wanted to make sure I got safely to work. We didn't talk about what happened just an hour before in Grand Island. I wanted to ask him about the money. I knew he worked, but most of his money was used to pay our bills and buy groceries.

The money I got from working at the diner wasn't a lot either, but I tried to help Jagger out as much as possible. We didn't get anything substantial out of the money we had. New clothes were rare and we had to make sure we didn't buy the most expensive meat for dinner.

When I got out of the car, Jagger told me he would be picking me up after my shift was over. I knew this had to do with Dean. Even if Jagger threatened him back at the police station not to come close to Hastings, I knew he wouldn't listen.

Jag knew too. That's why he was protecting me like this. Normally, he had let me walk home alone at night without being scared that something could've happened to me. And he was right about that. I always got home safe.

I was waiting for Hunter to show up at the diner. I started my shift at seven p.m. and I still had about fifteen minutes before I had to go in. I was staring at my phone, wondering if Hunter read my text.

"Oh, good. You're here too." I looked up, watching Adeline step out of her car and walking over to me. "Frankie texted me. He won't be here tonight so we have to close this place when we're done. And Elvis will only cook until eleven. He has to leave early too."

"Okay," I said, surprised that she still came around to work. Her makeup was freshly put on and her lipstick pretty much screamed for attention. She was pretty, yes. But I didn't understand the concept of makeup. To each his own, I thought.

"I've never really worked an evening shift. But Frankie said the tips get bigger the later it gets." She grinned, winked at me and then said, "This will be a fun evening." She then entered the diner through the back door.

I rolled my eyes, looking down at my phone again. It won't be fun. The men sitting there late at night were the worst. They were touchy, tried to lift my skirt several times, and asked me to sit on their laps for money multiple times. The thought of that made me shiver. "Disgusting," I whispered to myself.

"What is?" Hunter's voice startled me. I quickly

looked up, happy to see his face again. I tried to smile, but the sight of his busted nose made me drop my jaw instead.

"Oh, my…what happened?" I asked, walking toward him, wanting to take his face into my hands for a closer look. Instead of letting me do that, Hunter grabbed my waist and pulled me into his arms. I hugged him back, leaning into his chest and closing my eyes to take in this moment. I've missed him.

"Hey, sweetheart." He put his left hand on the back of my head, gripping my hair just enough to make it feel good.

"You just left this morning," I said into his sweater, frowning. I wasn't mad that he left. I was disappointed not to find him lying next to me, even if I wasn't sure he remembered anything he said to me.

"I know. Sorry about that." He loosened his arms slightly and pulled back just enough to look at me. His crooked grin was enough to forgive him. I studied his face for a moment.

"Who did this to you?" I asked quietly, hoping he would tell me. A busted nose meant he had a fight.

Hunter puckered up his lips, studying my face. Sighing, he brushed back one strand of hair behind my ear and said, "Jagger's fist landed in my face the second I stepped out of your room this morning."

My hand flew up and covered my mouth, keeping my eyes on his face. "Oh…"

"It's not that ba—"

He stopped, realizing I was about to start

laughing. "You think that's funny?" he asked, smirking and grabbing the back of my neck with his hand.

I let out a small laugh, still covering my mouth with my hand. I was about to burst out into laughter. I knew it was wrong, but imagining Jagger punching Hunter was just glorious.

"Jag punched you?" I said, now letting my hand fall to his chest and throwing my head back, laughing so hard my stomach started hurting. I couldn't remember the last time I laughed like this. Carefree and heartful. A real laugh. God, that made me feel so good!

"Fuck," he suddenly said and I stopped laughing immediately. Oh, no. Is he mad? I looked back up at him and he was watching me closely.

His hands came up to cup my face, his eyes fixed on my lips now. He said, "Your laugh is just as beautiful as you are."

Oh, my. My heart started beating faster than usual. That's when I realized it was the first time I laughed in front of him.

It was the first time our conversation was clean, easy, and fun. No drunken words were spoken. No slurring of words from his side and no confusion between the two of us.

It's not like I didn't believe the things he said to me last night. The words he said just now made more sense. He was present. His mind was clear and he had plenty of time and strength to think about the words he spoke.

"Do you really mean that?" I quietly asked. Seemed like I still needed reassurance. But that was probably because I wanted to hear him say it again.

He let out a small laugh, brushing his thumb over my bottom lip slowly and then nodding. "Hell, 'course I do."

His lips pressed against mine, holding my face firmly in his hands so I couldn't move away from him. Why would I, though? This was where I wanted to be. Close to him.

I held my breath, closing my eyes and pulling at his sweater to hold myself up. My knees felt weak and soft, as if they were about to give in.

I felt Hunter's tongue against my lips and I was more than happy to open up for him so I could taste him. I could tell he had been smoking before he came here, but that didn't bother me much.

It didn't bother me as much as Adeline, the moment she opened the back door and interrupted us.

CHAPTER TWENTY-FOUR

Harlow

"Don't mean to interrupt your hot make-out session, but I need you in here," Adeline said, smirking at me, then looking over at Hunter who still had his hands on my cheeks.

I pressed my lips together, lowering my head to look at Hunter's sweatshirt. I knew I was turning red for being caught making out with him. I couldn't decide whether or not to bury myself or just run and hide.

Hunter chuckled. "She'll be right there." He was amused by this. Perfect. I didn't want to get that kind of attention from anyone.

Adeline went back inside and I looked back up at Hunter, who now had a cocky grin on his face. "Relax, sweetheart. It's not like she caught us having sex."

"I know. It's just…" I sighed, shrugged, and then shook my head. "I have to go."

He nodded, kissing my forehead, and then taking

a step back. I immediately started missing him. I wanted him close. As close as possible. But I had to work and I wasn't sure he would want to stay here for over six hours, since today's one of the busier days and the diner would be open until after midnight.

"Jagger picking you up later?" he asked, shoving his hands into his pockets. He studied my face, wondering why he did that so often. But then, I liked looking at his face too. Even with a busted nose. It looked hot.

"Yeah," I said, tilting my head to the side. "When will I see you again?" Seems like my mouth couldn't just be quiet, instead, it said all the things that run through my mind when I'm with Hunter.

He smiled, shrugging. "Whenever you want to." He leaned back against his car. God, why did he have to be so charming? Now, I know all the things he has done to me before were not right. He hurt me. Mentally and physically. But he had his issues. I knew that. And no matter how hard this would be, I wanted to understand him and his mind. He was a mess. Lonely. And I liked him when he was all calm and sweet.

"Maybe I can come over to your place tomorrow after work."

And just like that, his face changed and the smile was gone. He raised an eyebrow, looking at me like I had just said something stupid.

"No," he simply said.

"Why not?" This was stressful. His changes in attitude were annoying. But I had to remind myself that everyone had their reasons for their words. I was still a bit hurt by his rejection.

"I said no. You gotta work." He nodded toward the back door of the diner. "I'll send you a text tomorrow."

I rolled my eyes. He was all cold and annoyed again. That was quick. I guess I gotta get used to that if I really wanted to find out about him and how his mind works.

"Don't roll your eyes at me," he warned before opening the car door and turning to look at me once more. "And stop frowning." His gaze lingered on me for a while, then he got into his car and drove off.

Great. The moment of happiness didn't last long and worry started to come up again. It seemed like he shut off any positive thoughts as soon as I triggered him with the wrong words.

Working at the diner last night wasn't as bad as I had imagined. Probably because Adeline was there and took all the attention off me. Lucky me. I still got some tips, though. Enough to finally be able to go grocery shopping today and stack up on two weeks' worth of lunch and dinner. Of course, Jagger and I tried to buy the least expensive things. Lots of canned food and only chicken for meat.

Jagger wasn't working today so after I came back home from school we went to the grocery store so we went to the grocery store before noon. I had written a list of the things we'd buy some years ago. We always got the same things because we knew it would be the cheapest way to buy the most products.

We never had any sodas or other special drinks.

Well, besides beer. Jagger needed it. Other than the beer Jagger drank, we drank water from the tap. It was free and unlimited. As long as we paid our bills, that is.

After we arrived back home, I put all the groceries away and hoped to talk to Jagger about the money he used to bail out Dean. But the second we got home, Jagger told me he had some things to handle and disappeared again.

What he did when he wasn't home or at work was none of my business. He made that clear a long time ago and I didn't ask him about it either. I knew I wouldn't get any answers from him. So, I just had to let it go.

It was getting dark and Jagger wasn't home yet. He texted me he would be home late and that I shouldn't wait on him for dinner. I made chicken soup, ate some of it, and put the rest in the fridge for Jag.

I've also been checking my phone more often than usual. Hunter didn't message me, even though he said he would last night. I had no reason to be mad at him. He had his own life and probably worked too. Not sure what he did, because he never told me. Jagger also never said a word about Hunter's work. And again, that was probably none of my business.

Still, I felt the need to check in on him. Make sure he was okay. He probably just forgot about me. But instead of sending him a text, I had the brilliant idea of going to the trailer park to visit him.

CHAPTER TWENTY-FIVE

Harlow

I've never been to the trailer park. It's located right at the city limit of Hastings, so I had a long walk ahead of me. Taking the bus wasn't an option since that would cost me money I would rather spend on something more needed. Walking wasn't a problem anyway and I had enough time to think about what possibly could go wrong visiting Hunter at his home.

I found out where he lived some years ago when Jagger told me he needed to go to the trailer park to help Hunter fix something. I also found out that day that Hunter didn't have any family in town. Well, he did have Bliss working at the diner out of town, so she probably lives close by too.

Knowing it was probably a bad idea going there, I forgot about Hunter possibly not even being there. What if he was at work? If he even had a job. No, he does have one. How would he be able to afford a car without any income?

I pushed the thought of Hunter being unemployed aside. It just seemed wrong to think about that. Even Jagger and I managed to have jobs.

The walk to the trailer park was longer than I had imagined. Even if I was walking at a normal pace, I was slowly getting a side stitch. I never worked out or did any kind of sports, so this was normal, I thought.

It was already getting dark out, not that Hastings would ever have the sun shining over it. At least it wasn't raining tonight. I liked it, but I had to walk back home after this and I wasn't sure I would want to get soaked.

I finally arrived at my destination and the first thing I saw before the entrance was a big sign made out of wood that had the word *T.P.* on it. Underneath it said in smaller letters: *Dogs bite, be cautious.*

"Great," I said, sighing and looking past the sign to the narrow path that led to all the trailers. To be honest, it didn't look that bad. Maybe this small community wasn't as bad as everyone said.

It took me a moment to start exploring, but when I did, I was quickly fascinated by the trailers. All of them were close to each other, some were painted in different colors, but most of them were just grey or white. Some of them had little gardens in the front with flowers and trees. Mud and puddles were common in this city but the T.P. had more than enough of it. I bet it's fun for kids to play here.

I found myself smiling at the thought of that and quickly realized that I was roaming around almost without any destination. I had to find Hunter's trailer. But how? There were no mailboxes around and I didn't see any names on the doors.

"You lookin' for something, sugar?" a male voice said behind me and I quickly turned to see who it was. A bold elderly man stood there, his chin high up in the air, looking down at me with narrowed eyes as if I was some sort of intruder. Theoretically, I was.

"Yes," I quickly answered, taking a step back just to get my personal space back. "I'm looking for Hunter."

The man laughed. "Of course you are." Then he nodded behind me. "Turn left at the end of this path. The teal one."

I nodded and thanked him before turning around and heading to where he just told me to go. *Of course you are*, what's that supposed to mean? Did he have lots of visitors? Hard to believe when Hunter himself told me not to come here yesterday. Or was it just me he rejected to come to visit him?

I stopped in my tracks and thought about that for a minute. What if he doesn't want me here? What if he wants to keep all of this to himself and not share his private life with me? I was thinking about myself too much without considering that Hunter might have his reasons why he didn't want me here.

I couldn't do this. He didn't want me here and I was invading his privacy when I was told no before. Why did I have to be so damn selfish all the time?

I shook my head, hating myself for standing here without an invitation. I quickly turned around again, walking back to the exit. The man who talked to me before was sitting in a chair in front of a trailer which was a dirty white color. He watched me as I passed him and raised an eyebrow before grinning. Great. Making a fool out of myself was becoming a talent of mine.

I ignored his funny stares and left the trailer park. I didn't stop but walked along the street to get back into town.

I was angry at myself. Angry that I thought I could just show up there and act like he wanted to see me there. Hunter didn't want to see me. Hell, he didn't even text me even if he said he would. I was too naïve. At least I was realizing that.

But it was still stupid. God, he didn't text.

He still hadn't texted and I was starting to think that he wouldn't do so anyway.

My mind was drifting off to a different place, keeping my head low and staring at the pavement underneath my feet. My thoughts were running wild and I had no intention of looking back or even up to see what vehicles were coming toward me with high speed into my direction.

And that was a mistake.

A loud honk, a voice shouting my name, something hitting my body with force and everything went black.

CHAPTER TWENTY-SIX

Hunter

Watching her body being hurled through the air after being hit by a car and landing in a ditch on the side of the road was terrifying. I had seen some shit along the way up until now but never had my mind and body gone numb from anything I've seen. The sight of her motionless body lying there hurt in a way I had never felt before. It shocked me to the point that my body felt sick and weak, and hell, not even the death of one of my best friends made me feel this way.

I felt sick to my stomach because I knew this happened because of me. Wilson knocked on my door to let me know a "*beautiful young girl*" asked for me just minutes before. I wasn't sure why any girl would ever look for me here. I never told anyone besides Jagger and a few other guys where I lived. Girls weren't allowed in my personal space. My own four walls I kept safe and secret from anyone. I never had girls over. That's not my style.

115

If I needed to let out some steam I would drive out of Hastings. But the last time was months ago.

But that was not the point. After looking at Wilson with a raised brow, he sighed and pointed to the exit of the T.P. and added, "Pretty eyes, long hair, freckles." And that sent me off running.

I had forgotten about her. Fuck! I forgot to text her. How the fuck did I forget about sweet Harlow?

I ran after her in the hopes she would still be in sight and I could catch her before she was too far gone. When I got to the street I immediately saw her walking at a fast pace back toward the city. Her body was tense and her head was low. I had made her upset without even talking to her. And her coming here had needed an explanation. Jagger must've told her. No other way she could've found out.

I called her name once but she didn't react. Probably didn't hear me. The cars were driving by fast and it was loud. I called her name again, this time louder. She kept on walking. She was either ignoring me, or she really didn't hear me. I couldn't imagine her ignoring me. I saw the way she looked at me and how her eyes lit up when she saw me. I knew something in her sparked the second she was close to me, and I'm not trying to flatter myself, but I knew her heart was set on me. Even after all I've done to her.

It was a way of defending myself. To keep her far away from me because I knew the second I let her get too close, I would break. I wasn't one for romance. I didn't get any growing up and I knew it was not something I deserved. Harlow knew what real love was. Jagger was her better half. The one guy in her life who showed her what real love was. He protected her and cared for her. He treated her like a damn princess and I knew I wasn't able to give her more than what her brother gave her all her life.

I knew it wasn't right to think all that. She had a miserable life too. She wasn't treated right as a child and she had to battle for a better life. But the thing is, she had someone who loved her now. She didn't need another man in her life who would probably just mess up and make it worse again. And I sure as hell wasn't going to be that man. No fucking way.

But still, here I was, sitting next to the hospital bed she was lying in, attached to a machine which helped her breathe.

The car hit her right in her upper body, crushing her thorax and smashing her lungs. I waited two hours in the waiting room before the doctors came out of the emergency room, telling me she would be okay.

I called Jagger to let him know about his baby sister getting hit by a fucking car right in front of my eyes and he rushed here. The terror in his eyes as he arrived in the waiting room was enough for me to hit rock bottom and feel like the last piece of shit on this planet.

Jagger sat on the other side of the bed, holding her hand tightly in his and letting tears roll down his face. Seeing him cry was a first. Jagger was always in a good mood. Mostly cheerful when he was around me and he never failed to make his sister smile. His sister who was lying in a hospital bed, with a mask over her face to help her breathe and a bandage around her upper body to stabilize her broken ribs. Two of them were broken. Luckily, her head wasn't injured. She wasn't in a coma. She received strong pain meds to help her sleep and I wasn't sure when she was going to wake up.

Yet, I didn't have any intention of leaving. The night had come and it started raining once again, as if the skies were crying too. But then, in Hastings, it always rained.

I knew that talking wasn't going to make him feel better but I needed him to know it would be okay. That his sister would make it through.

"She's strong. She'll make it through this," I said in a low voice, not to startle him. He was in deep thought, looking at Harlow's face. He reached up to her head with his right hand and caressed the side of her head carefully.

"I know," Jagger muttered with a shaky voice. "It's just the thought of losing her that scares the shit outta me."

I nodded, not being able to fully understand what it would feel like to have my sister lying here like this. Technically, Bliss wasn't my sister. She was adopted, just like me. We grew up in the same house but that didn't mean we had that connection that siblings had.

"I'm sorry, man."

He nodded, keeping his eyes on Low and running his fingers through her hair. "Yeah," he said slowly without giving me any attention. "Yeah, you should be."

CHAPTER TWENTY-SEVEN

Hunter

Jagger wasn't stupid. He knew Low was at the T.P. before being hit by that damn car. He knew she came to visit me and there was no way he would ever forgive me for not looking after his baby sister. His sister which he loved so much you could see it in his eyes. Just watching the way he looked at her with so much pride and never-ending love almost triggered jealousy at my end. I never looked at someone the way Jagger looked at her. And no one has ever looked at me that way, either.

I took full responsibility for what happened and I cursed myself for not being able to save her from this accident. I hated myself. She did not deserve this. Jagger didn't deserve it either. It was my fault and once again, I was the one who messed up.

My past was full of missteps and things I did wrong. Even at a young age, I was able to make people angry or frustrated with my actions. I've always been on the lookout to hit, break, or misuse

119

something or someone. I didn't care what others felt after I treated them like the last piece of shit, and I sure as hell didn't apologize for my maniac behavior. All of it felt right. The power I had in those moments was incredible and I craved it daily.

The way I treated Low was disrespectful, not only toward her but also her brother who I considered my best friend—if not brother. Watching him suffer from something I was responsible for hurt like hell.

I studied Jagger for a moment, waiting for him to say more, but after a few long minutes of silence, I got up from my chair and ran my hands through my already messy hair. "I'll get you some coffee and something to eat."

That was not going to make it better, but I figured if he wasn't going to leave his sister's side, the least I could do was bring him some food. I didn't even expect a *thank you* from him.

Taking one last look at Harlow, I sighed and walked out of the room. Closing the door silently behind me, I looked around to find an empty hallway. This hospital always made me feel sick. I'd spent some nights here getting stitches after fistfights and even got operated on once after being shot by some drug dealer from out of town who thought he could get more blow from me than he had paid for. Luckily, that bastard missed several times, but one bullet got stuck in my collarbone. He ran off after realizing that he had messed with the wrong guy and I was quick enough to let one of my guys know he was on the run. They caught him some blocks down the road and didn't think letting him live was the most appropriate thing to do. They shot him. No mercy. Just pure cruelty. And that cruelty lived inside of me too. Sweet Harlow had gotten a taste of it before and I was stupid enough to let her get too close.

I let out a curse and headed toward the elevators at the end of the hall. Before reaching them, a door opened and I turned to watch Jagger exit the room his sister was lying in and come toward me with so much determination it almost scared me. His fists were tight and the deep crease between his eyebrows was enough warning for me to brace myself for what was coming next.

"Forgive me, brother," he said in a shaky voice before his fist landed in my face. I stumbled back against the elevator, hitting my back against it with a loud thud. I knew this was coming. He was angry at me and I wasn't going to fight back. He could take as many hits at me as he thought were necessary to get back at me for what I let happen to his sister.

Another fist hit me right in the stomach and for a second I wasn't able to breathe. Damn, that was the worst feeling ever.

He didn't stop there. My face was his target and another fist hit my nose, right where he had punched me yesterday. I felt blood come out of the fresh wound, and before I could look up to see what his next punch was, his hard knuckles met my left eye. I felt it turn black instantly and I fell back against the elevator once more before hitting the ground and closing my eyes, now breathing heavily.

"Break it off, boys." A deep voice came our direction and I relaxed a bit, knowing there was nothing more coming from Jagger's outburst. "This is a goddamn hospital," the man said.

Jagger muttered, "No shit," before turning and walking back to Harlow's room.

I looked up, seeing the doctor who took care of Low when we arrived here standing in front of me. He held out his hand for me to take and I took it, letting him help me up. I wiped off some of the blood that ran down my nose and lips with the back of my hand.

"Did you deserve this?" he asked in an amused tone. He put his hand on my jaw, turning my head to look at my nose.

I let out a hard laugh. "Fuck, yeah, I did." He nodded, then touched my nose with his finger and thumb. "Let me stitch that up. You're lucky it's not broken." He then started walking toward a door and I followed him.

Hell, I deserved more than this and I know that if we wouldn't have been in a hospital, Jagger would've turned me into some sort of dead, lacerated pig. I was lucky today. Not sure he had let out all of his anger, but I knew I had to brace myself for more to come when we were out of here.

CHAPTER TWENTY-EIGHT

Harlow

Everything hurt. My body felt numb, yet the pain was rushing through my body in a way I'd never felt before. I tried to remember what happened. Why there was a mask over my mouth and nose pushing air into my lungs. My lungs hurt the most. Every breath I took was like a punch to my stomach, and each time I breathed out it felt like I wasn't going to be able to take in any air ever again. Luckily, the machine helped.

I kept my eyes closed, wondering if I was dreaming. I was too scared to look so I tried to think about what had put me in such pain.

My name being called was what came to mind first, then a sharp pain from something heavy hitting me. A car. I got hit by a car. And it happened because I was walking away from something. My brows furrowed, remembering what the reason was why I wasn't careful while walking on the side of the road.

Then, Hunter's face was in front of me. I went to the trailer park to see him. I wanted to make sure he was okay, but the closer I got to his home, the more I realized what I was doing was stupid. So I turned and left without looking back. Without seeing him.

I felt something on my left hand, squeezing gently. *You can open your eyes now*, I thought. This was real. I was awake and alive. Taking in another painful breath, I slowly opened my heavy eyes and looked up to the ceiling. It was dark in this room and the beeping of the machines told me I was lying in a hospital bed. I was safe.

"Hey, sweet girl," I heard my brother's voice whisper before I turned to look at him. He was sitting next to the bed, one of his hands holding mine tightly and the other coming up to brush over my head. His tired smile and red eyes said it all. He had been crying and hadn't slept in a while.

I closed my eyes again for a second, adjusting to the moonlight beaming through the window behind Jagger. When I opened them again, I tried to squeeze his hand back, but I just didn't have enough strength in my body.

"Are you okay?" I asked quietly through the mask, which just made my voice sound muffled. I regretted speaking, though, because my lungs tightened at my attempt to use words.

Jagger let out a small laugh, shaking head. "You're the one in a damn hospital bed and you ask me if I'm okay? Hell, Low, you fascinate me each damn day."

I tried to smile but I knew he wasn't okay. I accepted pain fast and I didn't like other people being hurt. I reached up to touch the mask, trying to figure out if I could take it off. It wasn't comfortable and the sound it made wasn't that nice either.

"Don't," Jagger said, grabbing my hand and laying it back to my side. "I'll call the doc. Tell him you're awake." I slowly nodded, closing my eyes again and trying to inhale as slowly as possible. I heard Jagger move, then something clicked and he sat back down, taking my hand in his once again.

"You're incredibly strong, you know that?" he asked, caressing the back of my hand with his thumb. I tried to smile but nodded instead. I knew I was. But so was he. He taught me strength and how to live.

"I was hoping you would let me sleep through the night, but I guess you waking up already is good too." The unfamiliar voice came closer after a door closed. The humor and amusement in it told me I could trust him.

"Told you she's a fighter." Jagger chuckled and I finally opened my eyes again. A man, probably in his fifties, stood on the other side of the bed and looked down at me with a hint of relief in his eyes. I couldn't quite read the name on his white coat but I thought it wasn't necessary to know his name for now.

"Glad you're awake. I'll go through some check-ups." He handed me some sort of clicker. "Click if something hurts when I touch it, all right?" he said and I nodded. I looked back at Jagger, who looked a bit more relaxed. He was still holding my hand to reassure me that he wasn't going anywhere. I knew he wouldn't, but I knew he felt better if he could let me know he was here.

The doc switched on a dimmed light and started checking the machines first, and once in a while more air than needed pushed into my lungs. It didn't hurt, it was just a weird feeling. I looked back at him, now being able to read his name. Dr. Sullivan. That sounded nice. And he seemed to be good at his job. So I closed my eyes and let him do his thing, without clicking once.

"All looks good so far. I want to keep you here for another two days, just to make sure everything heals perfectly and your lungs won't give in without that mask." He wrote something onto his clipboard, then looked back at me.

"This is totally up to you," he then said, giving me a smile. "But there's someone waiting for you outside who wants to see you. Now, I know your brother already handled his part of this, but I think this is your call now." He looked over at Jagger and I did the same.

Handled what?

Jagger let go of my hand, rubbing his right hand with his left. That's when I saw the bruises on his knuckles and I couldn't stop myself from rolling my eyes. He punched Hunter. Again.

I raised an eyebrow at him, letting him know I disapproved of that kind of behavior. Jagger shrugged, looking down at his hands. "He owed me for this, Low. I wasn't that hard on him." Dr. Sullivan let out a laugh and put the clipboard with my medical notes into the little holder at the end of my bed. "He looks worse than you think. That boy let you hit him without fighting back." He then looked at me. "That's something to think about if you ask me."

Chapter Twenty-Nine

Hunter

My face was burning from Jagger's punches and I told myself to just accept all the pain I had right at that moment. I deserved it. All of it. But not just the pain Jagger caused but also the one I triggered myself by being a fucking idiot. I should've just texted her. I was stupid, forgetting about her when I damn well knew she'd probably come looking for me. Because that's what sweet Harlow did. She checked on people. She cared about people. Even me. And I sure as hell didn't deserve any of it.

I was staring at my phone, still sitting in the waiting room of the hospital for any news on Harlow. On the screen, it said "*7 missed calls from Harlow.*" She had tried to call me seven fucking times yesterday. Four times in the morning and three times in the afternoon. And I had ignored her calls. Well, in the morning I did. For my defense, I had turned my phone to "do not disturb" after eleven a.m. I had been getting other texts from

128

some people I didn't want to hear from. But that was a shit move.

I started reading her texts.

Harlow: Do you still want to see me today?

The other text was simply my name with a question mark. I hated how unsure she was, asking me if I still wanted to see her. She thought she was to the reason I didn't answer her. That she was the one who did something wrong. Hell, she thought it was her fault that I didn't answer.

Selfless. That's one way to describe sweet Harlow. So fucking selfless. Combine that with her striking beauty and you will not be able to keep your eyes and mind off her.

That day I told her she was beautiful inside and out, she had even questioned that. She was a smart girl, but seeing her clueless and unsure about what I had said made me think. Had no one ever told her how amazing she was? Guys surely didn't look away when she passed them. They'd be stupid not to want to get to know her. Fuck, I knew I wanted to get close to her the second I laid eyes on her. But that was years ago. She wasn't even eighteen yet and the thought of an underage Harlow was just wrong. She was older now. She had turned into a stunning young woman with legs that could make any girl jealous and a body that made every guy want a taste. No, let me rephrase that. A body that every guy would want a taste of if they had fucking functional eyeballs in their heads. Turns out no one ever tried to get close to her. Or she was just good at turning men down. Either way, I was closer than I should've ever allowed myself to be but I wasn't going to back away now. Not after what happened. I had to make it up to her.

"Apologize to her, then go home." Jagger's voice broke through my thoughts and I looked up, seeing him standing in the doorway to the waiting room.

"Damn." He let out a chuckle that didn't sound genuine. "Maybe I should get back to fighting." He was studying my face and the way he disfigured my nose. I was pretty sure my nose was crooked from the two times he punched it. I didn't fight much, but when I did, I was mostly the one who got away without any bruises or bloody wounds. Jagger was a pro. He did some underground fighting some years ago to earn some money, but he stopped as soon as Harlow started worrying about him. She saw her brother's face all red and blue and started asking questions. He told me he couldn't take her concerned frowns and tears when he got back home all beaten up. He stopped because of her and that was the first time I realized how much he loved his sister. And how much she cared about her brother's health.

"Don't think she would like that," I said, standing up from my seat and shoving my phone into my pocket. He knew I was talking about Harlow.

He nodded. "I know." He sat down in the nearest seat and ran his hands through his hair.

"She'll be okay. Doc wants to keep her here for a couple of days but she'll be up on her feet again." I wasn't sure why he was telling me all this. He should be hating me. Hell, he should be telling me not to see his sister ever again or even end our friendship. But then I thought about the way Harlow treats people. Jagger was just like her. Forgiving. Good. Selfless.

I nodded slowly, not sure if I should say something. It felt wrong to talk or try to make him feel better. He didn't need me to crawl up his ass to show him I was sorry. So I started toward the hallway.

"Hey, man," Jagger said and I turned to look back at him. "Yeah?"

He looked up at me, his eyes were dark and tired from too little sleep. "Whatever she sees in you, and whatever you two have…" he started. I braced myself for the worst. He was going to tell me not to see her ever again. To basically fuck off and not even think about Harlow again. In the end, I deserved it. So whatever he was going to say, I would accept it. I would walk into that hospital room, apologize to sweet Harlow, and then leave. Not sure how I would cope with that but I would at least try. For Jagger. And fuck, for Harlow's sake too.

"Don't fuck it up. Don't break her. She's the only one I got, and the next time you fuck up I'm not gonna hold back."

CHAPTER THIRTY

Hunter

I imprinted Jagger's words into my brain, just to make sure I would always remember them. He had every right in this world to tell me what to do and not to do when it came to his sister, and just seconds ago he indirectly told me that he accepted me around Harlow, even after what happened.

I knocked on the door of her room and then opened it slowly, taking in a sharp breath. As I stepped inside, Harlow's eyes were on me instantly. Seeing her like this was breaking my heart in millions of pieces. Sure, I saw her some hours ago when she was asleep and that hurt too, but now that she was awake and looking at me with those beautiful eyes of hers, I knew I had just one chance to apologize to her for being a massive fuck-up.

I closed the door behind me, not taking my eyes off hers. I sat down in the chair next to her bed. The breathing mask she had on earlier was gone but now a nasal breathing tube was fixed under her nose and tugged behind both of her ears. Even with that thing on her face, she was the most beautiful girl I'd ever seen. Her skin was pale, her freckles darker than usual, and her lips were a soft pink color, plump and swollen.

She studied me while I let my eyes travel over her face. I knew I was supposed to be the one to speak first, but my thoughts were running wild. I had so much to say. So many things I wanted her to know. But I wanted to say the right things. I had to reflect on my words.

Her breathing was calm and steady. Dr. Sullivan had told us about her broken ribs and collapsed lung. He wasn't sure how long it would take for her to be able to breathe without pain. The pain I caused.

I looked back into her eyes. Her gaze was steady, never leaving mine. I could see all kinds of emotions in them. She was unsure, but the flash of kindness in her eyes let me know that she was okay with me being here. Hell, there was even concern in her eyes. She saw the stitched up nose and my black eye, and she was fucking worried about *me* when *she* was the one who got hit by a damn car. But reading her was easy. Her eyes were so damn expressive.

When I gathered all my thoughts and was sure to be able to form normal sentences, I reached up with my hand to cup her face, caressing her cheek with my thumb. I was scared she would turn her head or flinch, instead, she leaned more into my hand, closing her eyes for a split second.

"I don't deserve you," I said, my voice low. Her

eyes were back on mine. This time, tears stung her eyes and I was so fucking close to finishing what Jagger had started and put myself into more pain. I hated seeing her cry. "I know that nothing I'm going to say will ever make up for this or make you forgive me, but I want you to hear me out. I'm sorry for treating you the way I did. I've been cruel. You deserve so much, and a guy should worship the damn ground you walk on." I stopped, holding my breath because I realized that nothing I was saying made any sense. Nothing came out the way I wanted it to and I was messing up again.

"Fuck," I said, letting out a small, hard laugh. "Can't you just tell me to fuck off and never see you again? Because I know damn well I won't be able to keep my distance. I want to hold you. I want to be so damn close to you it hurts. And even if I did the worst job of protecting you, I want to keep you safe." I was rambling now and I sounded even more stupid than before.

Her eyes never left mine and she didn't say a word. She wasn't going to talk. She was probably just letting me talk to make me feel better. This was full-on chaos and torture for me.

"I'm sorry," I said and got up from my seat, running my hands through my hair. "Stay," she simply said, surprising me. I wondered if it would be a good idea to stay. I didn't have anything to say that was good enough. I was starting to hate myself more and more.

"Please, stay," she repeated in a weak voice. I battled my thoughts for a second, then decided to just sit my ass down and listen to what she had to say. I was hoping for her to throw something negative at me to make me feel bad. I needed her to call me names. To tell me what an asshole I was.

"Do you remember that night you were in my bed, drunk?" she asked, her voice almost breaking at her effort to speak up.

I nodded slowly. "Of course I do." And that was the truth. I had been drinking but I also told her I would remember that night forever.

"You said we were a mess." She took a deep breath that made her frown. Breathing hurt her and she wasn't able to keep that from me. I reached for her hand and she let me take it. My need to touch her never left me. She studied me again, now battling her thoughts about what to say.

"I want to start over. You said you want to hold me and keep me close, but I don't think that will work out if you won't let me get close to you. If you really want this—us—you have to open up to me."

Opening up to her sounded like a bad idea. I had a past full of violence, hatred, and mistakes. Jagger knew some about it but even he didn't get to hear the full story. I slowly shook my head.

"That would only push you away, sweetheart, and I'm not sure I want that."

She shrugged. "That's something I will have to decide." She was right on that. The things I told Jagger only welded us together and made our friendship stronger. Because I knew about his past too.

I sighed, letting my head fall and running my hands through my hair. "One step at a time?" I asked, looking back up into that beautiful face of hers. She nodded, giving me a small, tired smile. I relaxed a bit, knowing she was going to give me another chance.

"This is my fault," I said, nodding to her injured body. "I promise you I will be better. I will make it all so much better."

"I'm alive, Hunter. I will be fine." I smiled at that, her strength and positivity amazing me each damn time. I pulled her hand to my mouth, kissing the back of it while keeping my eyes on hers. "You're incredible."

She nodded, telling me she was well aware of that. She should be. Nothing but the truth in that.

CHAPTER THIRTY-ONE

Harlow

Jagger entering the room was probably what I needed. I was getting drawn into Hunter's charming words again too quickly and I told myself, and him, to take it slow this time. We had a lot to figure out, and him giving me that sweet smile of his and the way he touched me was making me feel all types of ways. I needed to approach this at a normal pace. The last time I let him get close I was head over heels and I couldn't think straight. I let him get to me, so close I wasn't sure how to handle his whole being. He had issues. I figured that out some time ago, but I never had the guts to ask him about it. His anger and hurtful words and way of treating me were enough to keep me quiet, yet not enough to keep me away from him.

When it came to Hunter, I just couldn't think straight. I wanted him close but I also wanted to shout at him and tell him to get away from me. Something in his eyes told me that he needed someone to look after him. Someone who cared about him.

"Doc wants us gone," Jag said, looking at Hunter, then turning his gaze to me. "I'll come by in the morning. You need some rest." It was already way past midnight and I knew Jagger and Hunter were up all night, not getting any sleep since the accident happened. I felt Hunter's hand squeeze mine and I turned to look at him. He had a deep crease in his forehead, telling me he wasn't ready to leave me alone.

"You two need some sleep too." I looked back over at Jagger, who had his arms crossed over his chest and a disapproving frown on his face. "We've talked about this, okay?" I sighed, now frowning back at him. "I can't keep him out of my life. We talked and we're figuring things out. I'm a big girl, Jag. I know what I'm doing. You gotta trust me."

"I trust you, sweet girl. It's him I'm not so sure about." He nodded his head toward Hunter, keeping his eyes on me.

"He messed up a couple of times. He's been an ass most of the time, but there is something that keeps me from running from him. I have no idea why my heart and mind want him near, but he needs me. He's broken. And even if I don't quite understand why I want to be the one to fix him, I can't push myself away from him. He's your friend. He needs you too." I looked back at Hunter. His eyes were full of shame and slight anger. Good. He needed to hear me say all that to realize that I'm not blind. I saw how much he's hurting inside and I was going to help him conquer it.

"Now, both of you stop acting like you're at my funeral and get out of here. I'll see you tomorrow." Talking that much hurt my lungs. But I had to get it out there even if I wasn't making much sense.

"And no more fighting," I warned Jagger. His frown was growing for a second but it quickly turned into a grin he couldn't hold back. He shook his head, letting his arms fall to his side. "Damn, sis, what the hell has gotten into you?"

Hunter let out a chuckle, patting my hand before he got up from his seat.

"I think I gotta be more scared for you than for her, man," Jag said, looking back at Hunter. He nodded, bending down to kiss my lips softly. "Rest, love. See you tomorrow," he whispered, then walked over to the door. Jagger took two steps toward the bed, then bent down to kiss the top of my head before saying he loved me and wishing me a good night.

I watched them both exit the room, wondering how I was so lucky to have two men in my life who actually cared. Well, Jagger always did. He was my rock, my home, my everything since the day I was born. But it was new to me to have Hunter and knowing he wouldn't let go of me. He had told me he wanted me close. I believed him. No doubt in that.

I couldn't fall back asleep after they left and I was battling to just stay awake for the rest of the night or force myself to sleep. Maybe some television would help. I reached for the remote next to my bed and turned on the TV, switching channels a few times before leaving it on some cartoons. I didn't watch lots of TV at home, but I knew this show was called *Archer*.

Just as I put the remote down, my phone vibrated, and I picked it up to look at the message written on my screen.

Hunter: Still awake?

I smiled at his text and quickly started typing a reply when a soft knock came from the door. I turned, thinking it would be a nurse or Dr. Sullivan to check on me but the second I saw Hunter's head peek through, I found myself smiling even wider.

"What are you doing here?" I asked.

"You really think I'm going to let you stay in this hospital all alone?" He walked over to me, grabbing my face into his hands and gently kissing me. That was it. I didn't care if he was allowed to be here or that I've told him to leave just a while ago. I wanted him here.

"You're crazy," I mumbled into the kiss.

He grinned, pulling away to look me in the eyes. "You have no idea how fucking crazy I am about you, love."

CHAPTER THIRTY-TWO

Hunter

Having her in my arms was all I needed after everything that happened. I wasn't supposed to be here. Jagger was gone and told me to go home, but I wasn't ready to let Low stay all by herself in the hospital. It was also in the middle of the night and she probably needed some more sleep, yet she was snuggling up to me as close as her pain would let her.

She pulled me down next to her and told me to lie down with her. I was hesitant, not wanting to hurt her or take her space, but she almost threatened me that if I wouldn't lay down with her she would push the button on the head of her bed to call Dr. Sullivan. She was pretty stubborn and I realized that I'd be better off pleasing her and not piss her off.

I've been over that. I've pushed her limits multiple times and it ended in her either crying, being mad, or doubting herself. I didn't want any of those things, so I just gave in and carefully lay

141

down next to her.

I turned, lying on my side and reaching my hand up to cup her face. She was still on her back, just turning her head to me and letting her eyes wander over my face. Every time she did that, she started to chew on her bottom lip. Her brows would furrow from time to time and her eyes showed different emotions every other second. It was like there was a battle in her brain, trying to figure out her next move. Fascinating as hell, which only confirmed my theory of being able to read her well.

"What's going on in that pretty little head of yours, love?" I asked in a whisper, brushing her hair back and tugging it behind her ear. She kept her eyes on me, looking at my lips for a while before they came back up to meet my eyes.

"Tell me about your childhood," she said, making my head spin with memories flashing through my mind at high speed. This was coming, and I knew if I wanted to keep her close to me, I needed to open up. Still, I wasn't sure I could just go on and tell her about every little thing that had happened to me when I was a kid. My past was full of missteps and maltreatment. I hated to talk about it. But then, I knew about her past without her knowing and that wasn't fair.

I studied her the same way she always studied me for a while before taking a deep breath. I leaned into her, taking her lips and gently kissing them. I needed another taste. I was scared that she would push me away because my life before Hastings was scary and miserable. This town changed me and made me realize many things.

She opened her mouth just enough to let me slip my tongue inside her mouth to get some more of her sweetness. Fuck me. How was I supposed to ever let go of her? We never had sex. The most I've seen of her were her tits. Best fucking tits I ever got to kiss and suck on. But if just kissing her made me want to act like a mad man, banging my fists against my chest like a crazed man, I don't know how I could ever be without her.

Her hand came up to touch my neck and the sweetest little noise broke out from her as I grabbed a fistful of her hair at the back of her head. I felt her hips move against me and her other hand reached down to grab my shirt right at the hem, telling me she wanted much more. She wasn't the only one, though.

"If you weren't injured and in a hospital bed, I would make you feel so good, sweetheart." My lips still touched hers as I said those words and I couldn't help but grin the second a whispered moan escaped her.

"Hunter," she mumbled, grabbing my shirt with her hand. "You didn't answer me."

At this point, I wasn't sure I could stop myself from this. She was enjoying me saying those things while touching and kissing her.

Taking a small nip at her bottom lip, I let my hand run through her hair again, tugging on it just enough to hear that moan again. "You don't really want me to stop," I said, knowing exactly what her answer to that would be. "That night I spent in your bed…" I started kissing her neck. "I was so damn drunk but I knew I had to hold myself together. I was battling my fucking head not to slip a hand down those sweet pajama pants you had on. I was so damn close to ripping them off, but I knew I had to play nice."

I felt her shiver next to me and now her hand gripped my hair, pulling tight at the ends and making me look up to see her face full of lust and desire. We were in a damn hospital bed and she was worked up just by my dirty talk. I liked it. And I knew she did too. So why stop there? The past can wait. This was not a place I wanted to talk about my fucking past. I needed her all to myself, cuddled up with me on her bed.

"Right now, I would love to do just that. Slip my hand down your panties and make you feel so good, love."

Another moan escaped her.

"But I don't wanna hurt you, you know?" I kissed her lips again, exploring her mouth with my tongue and letting her pull my hair as hard as she wanted. "You think you can wait? Wait until you're all fixed up and strong again?" Looking back into her eyes, I saw the frustration in them. I knew what she wanted, but it wasn't going to happen. And she knew that too.

"I think so," she whispered.

That made me chuckle. "I hope so, sweetheart. Breathing is an important part of orgasms and your pretty lungs aren't strong enough for that just yet."

CHAPTER THIRTY-THREE

Harlow

I couldn't take more of his teasing. Even with all the pain, my body was on fire and my heart was beating faster than ever. Even the machine I was attached to was making weird noises, probably because my breathing sped up too. I was hoping it wasn't the nurse's turn to come in and check on me yet.

Hunter's words made me feel warm and fuzzy inside and I could feel the wetness down there. The way he used his words was new to me. He was very blunt with them before but he never actually used them in a sexual way toward me. He cussed a lot, said *fuck* or *fucking* multiple times in a conversation. That didn't bother me at all. But hearing him say those words, telling me what he wanted to do with me and my body so precisely made me wonder if he used those words with other girls too. If he had ever told a girl how wet her panties were and wanting to make them orgasm.

145

No, I wasn't about to get jealous about that. He was with me. Why bother thinking about him and other girls?

"Harlow, love, you with me?" he asked, leaning over me.

I nodded, realizing I had spaced out while he was kissing my neck and trying to keep up with his words.

"Would it be that exhausting? I mean...the orgasm?" I asked in a whisper, almost too afraid to speak up or even say that word.

Hunter's smile grew wide. "You've never had an orgasm," he said, not even putting it in a question because he knew already that it was the truth. I shrugged, embarrassed by my inexperience.

"Sweetheart," he started, brushing a strand of hair back and tugging it behind my ear. His eyes went dark and his tongue came out to lick his lips. God, he was just too damn handsome.

"As much as I would like to taste your sweetness, I really don't think you could handle any of it. I need you naked and unhurt. I need to be able to play with those sweet tits of yours while I suck on your clit and play with your pussy. And I need to hear you scream my name and make those heavenly sounds you make as loud as possible. But that's not gonna happen in a damn hospital bed, with you injured and all wrapped up in bandages."

Holy shit.

Just hearing him say all that made me shiver all over again and I wasn't sure if I should stop him because it was pure torture, knowing none of what he said would be happening anytime soon.

146

I tried to form words but I just couldn't. I hoped my eyes would express how much I wanted him to do everything he said just then. I was desperate. God, since when did I become so horny?

All thanks to him, I thought.

"You gonna talk to me, love?" he asked, grinning and knowing exactly how much he was teasing me. His fingers softly traced a line down along the side of my neck.

I just nodded, unable to say anything. I felt like I was out of breath but my lungs seemed not to hurt anymore. If anything, he was distracting me from the pain with his words, which was kind of nice.

"Someone's speechless," he teased, watching me and not letting his eyes leave mine. "I really don't want to hurt you, you know?"

"I know," I blurted out fast, hating myself for acting like some sort of sex-hungry person. I was now even using words that didn't make sense. My brain was going blank again and I wasn't thinking straight. *I wish I was out of this bed.*

Hunter let out a small chuckle, amused by all of this.

"You should rest, Low." Something in his voice changed and he suddenly sounded serious.

"Are you leaving?" I sounded desperate. He only just came back and now he wanted to leave already?

"Not going anywhere, love." He smiled and pushed himself up with one hand and stood back up. He looked down at me and ran his fingers through my hair. "I'm staying here. Well, for as long as I possibly can. I don't think the nurses will be pleased seeing me here past visiting hours." He looked around the room, and despite what he just said, he sat down in the chair next to the bed.

"I'll stay until someone kicks me out."

I let out a laugh and shook my head. "I'd love to see someone kick you out of here. Would be the first time you ever did something you're told."

"Ouch," Hunter exclaimed and put his hand on his chest, showing me just how hurt he was by my comment. "Someone's feisty." He chuckled and I grinned, happy to be able to joke around like that with him.

CHAPTER THIRTY-FOUR

Harlow

We looked at each other in silence while Hunter held my hand in his, stroking the back of it. After some time, I had to pick up on what I started. He had yet to answer my question.

"Will you ever tell me about your past?" I asked, pretty much destroying this whole vibe. But I was desperate to know. I couldn't stand knowing he was holding all of those negative things inside of him when he could easily open up and trust me. Maybe he needed reassurance.

"You can talk to me, okay? I know it's hard to talk about the past…I hate it too. But I would like to know who you are, Hunter." I bit my bottom lip, hoping he wasn't going to get mad. God, I shouldn't. The last time I tried to get close to him in any way I got hit by a car.

"You don't have to tell me everything. I just want you to know that I'm here. If you need me…" I took a small break, swallowing my last piece of courage. "I'm here for you and I trust you."

"Stop," he interrupted, shaking his head. *Great. Shit. Shit!*

"I'm sorry, I—"

"Damn it, Low, stop," he commanded, gripping my neck a little too firmly.

He eyed my face for a while, my breathing suddenly getting heavier. There was that fear again. His angry outbursts were nothing new and I knew how to handle them now but I wasn't sure I wanted him to get all fired up in a hospital. Other patients didn't need to be woken up, and as long as the nurses didn't come in, I wanted to keep him here with me for as long as possible.

After some seconds, which felt like minutes, he sighed. "I don't deserve you caring about me so much. I don't want you to care. But I know if I keep you out like that for any longer I will probably lose you and I'm not fucking having that."

Oh, so he wasn't mad?

"You're too damn sweet. I have no clue why the fuck you even keep up with me after everything I've done to you. Even after this…" he said, looking down to my body and shaking his head once again. "I know I'm the last person on this planet to ever deserve you, but I'm a selfish bastard and you're all I want. I know I've been an idiot. Hell, I've been a motherfucking asshole toward you."

He looked back into my eyes, squeezing my hand. "I don't make any sense most of the time but please, love, don't ever run from me. And if you do run, I will catch you."

He was right about all that. He was an asshole.

150

Rude and cruel at times and he treated me like I was nothing. But he was also begging just then. Begging for me not to ever let him stand alone. My heart melted and my body was getting warm all over. This man had no idea what he was triggering inside of me with those words. I wanted to tell him exactly how I felt and my thoughts were running wild again. But it was too early. I couldn't tell him how much I felt for him. That was wrong. No, not wrong. It was too soon. I'd once heard a girl at the diner talk to her friend who was crying about a boy and she said something along the lines of "that's why you always wait for *him* to say I love you first."

That was probably bullshit, but I wasn't going to risk it. I was sure about my feelings for Hunter, but I yet had to find out what he was really thinking about me. About us.

I smiled at him, squeezing his hand too. "I don't really like running," I said jokingly. I was hoping to lighten up his mood. God, didn't he have any idea that he had a good side to him too?

Hunter let out a laugh. "You're too damn adorable, you know that?"

"Heard it before, yes."

He shook his head with a genuine grin on his face, bending over to kiss my lips softly. After a few seconds, he let go and touched his stitched up nose to mine. "There's no way in hell I will ever let go of you. I promise you that."

"Good, and I won't leave," I assured him, closing my eyes. "As much as I would like to talk to you, I don't think I can stay awake any longer," I added.

Hunter kissed the tip of my nose and then my forehead. Right before he was going to say something, the door opened and I heard Hunter sigh.

The nurse looked at us, then she took a glance at her watch and made an annoyed sound. "I'm sorry, but I will have to ask you to leave, sir."

I bit back a grin, turning my head to look back at Hunter. He wasn't hiding his amusement and got up from his chair to bend down one last time. "Don't enjoy this too much," he whispered against my lips before kissing them.

"I'll see you tomorrow." I nodded, smiling at him one last time before watching him leave the room.

"Sorry about that," I said to the nurse, now feeling guilty for annoying her. She shrugged it off with a fake smile. "It's nothing new, darling."

CHAPTER THIRTY-FIVE

Hunter

Leaving her alone felt wrong, but she had to get some rest. It was nice staying with her, being near her and making sure she was doing okay. I told her that I didn't deserve her. I've been treating her like shit and her just pushing aside my cruel behavior like that made me realize what kind of a person she was.

Her heart was bigger than anyone's I've ever met before. Her genuine eyes and her acceptance toward all kinds of people made me almost sick to my stomach, knowing I've messed with her like that. She saw the good in people, letting them know just how much she cared about them, and I most certainly wasn't one of those who should be even knowing a kind, precious girl like that.

I've never done anything good in my life. I always fucked up and rarely got shit right unless it was something horrible. I was good at fucking up. It was almost like a gift God gave me but I wasn't so

153

sure why the hell he wouldn't punish me for it. Instead, he gave me the best gift I could've ever wished for. Harlow. She was all I wanted right now.

I was hoping Jagger wouldn't find out that I went back for her last night. He has been through enough stuff and I wasn't going to piss him off once again. And another beating wasn't in my schedule.

The next morning I arrived at the hospital before visiting hours and my body instantly ached for her presence. I had to remind myself that I still had balls. Fuck, I was so damn pussy-whipped. No girl has ever made me feel this way and I only just realized that Harlow was the only one who could make me feel all warm and tingly inside.

Jesus Christ, Hunter! Man up!

After a quick stop in the restroom, I took the elevator to the first floor and went ahead to grab me a black coffee in the cafeteria. That was exactly what I needed. A strong, bitter reminder that I couldn't just go all soft because of her. I had shit to handle which didn't have anything to do with sweet Harlow but required a focused mind and strength. After all, my job wasn't for the weak.

I sat down in a chair, leaning back and taking a long sip from my coffee. Caffeine was another thing I was lacking big time. Last night I was up until the early morning and I wasn't thinking about sleep. Instead, my mind was filled with thoughts of Harlow.

My phone vibrated in my pocket and I pulled it out, reading a familiar name on the screen. Sighing, I tried to guess what was written in that message. I had set my notifications to just show the name of the messenger, without revealing the content of the text. I didn't need others to randomly read my texts. They were my business.

Not opening it wasn't an option, and running from him or ignoring him would put me into deep shit. I wasn't going to mess with him. Or his people.

I slid my thumb over the screen, punching in my password and letting the message pop up.

Text: 10

It simply said a number and I knew what it meant. Perfect. Something new was coming up but I wasn't sure I was able to work with Harlow being in the hospital.

"You got the text?" Jagger's voice broke through my thoughts about his baby sister and I looked up at him. He didn't get much sleep himself and he still had that angry gleam in his eyes. All of this was probably getting to him.

"Yeah," I answered, pushing my phone back into my pocket. "You're here early." I drank my coffee and threw the cup into the bin next to my table.

He looked at me with a cocked eyebrow, letting me know that it was a stupid thing to say. Then he let his eyes wander down to my feet and back up, eyeing my face carefully. "You been here all night?" he asked.

"No, I just couldn't really sleep. I wish I could've stayed with her all night."

I decided that honesty was the only right thing at this point. Jagger slowly nodded, not really approving of it.

"I hope you remember my words. I'm not trying to play games here, Kane. I hope you know what you're doing."

"Trust me," I said, standing up and running my hands through my hair. "She's changing me. She got me all wrapped up around her little finger and fuck, man…" I let out a hard laugh. "I'll be the one not making it out alive. She's got my whole heart. At least what's left of it. I need her close. She knows that."

Jagger's confused and almost amused look was what I deserved at that moment. I was talking like a crazed man, and I sure as hell wasn't making any sense. But he seemed to understand.

"What the fuck does she even see in you?"

That made me laugh because I didn't know either.

"If I ever find out, I'll tell you."

CHAPTER THIRTY-SIX

Harlow

Jagger and Hunter were both standing next to my bed really early in the morning. When I woke up, the sun was barely out and both of them looked at me with a sad, tired smile. I wondered if they ever closed their eyes last night.

"Did you get some sleep?" I asked, reaching out my hand to grab Jagger's. He shrugged, knowing that he couldn't lie to me. He sat down in the chair he sat in yesterday and patted the back of my hand with his other.

"Don't worry about me." He let out a sigh, looking up at Hunter for a second. "Since we're all here, I think you two gotta explain all of this to me. I'm not gonna be an ass and get in the way of whatever you two have," he said, looking back into my eyes, concerned. "But I have told him before. If he ever fucks up, you tell me and I will end him."

The way he said it sounded amusing but I knew he wasn't joking. He meant every word of it and he was warning Hunter. But also me, since it takes two to tango. Hunter heard a talk like this from him before and he also got a beating out of it. He knew he had to follow Jagger's rules and commands right now.

"Now, what's going on exactly?" he asked, keeping his eyes on me. I quickly looked up at Hunter, not knowing how to answer that question. What *was* going on? I mean, we hung out for a bit in the last few weeks and we kissed. He also touched me a lot and told me more than one time that he wanted and needed me close. But that didn't clarify anything.

I was clueless as to what to call it. Were we friends or already dating? We sure as hell weren't in a relationship.

"We're figuring things out," Hunter said, looking back at me. "Well, I'm figuring things out." He turned to look at Jagger, shoving his fists into his pockets.

"You know I got some shit going on right now and I don't want her anywhere close to that. I'm looking for a way out so I can keep her with me more often. I'd like to take her out, go on dates and just…" He stopped, looking back at me. "Letting her get to know me. That's what she deserves."

My heartbeat sped up and my cheeks warmed. God, who was this person looking like Hunter? He seemed changed. But like he said, he had things to handle he didn't want me to know about.

"A way out?" Jagger said, lifting an eyebrow. He didn't seem too impressed with that. But a way out of what? I still had no idea what they were doing to earn money. The only thing I could imagine them doing was drug dealing. It's dangerous and illegal. That's why they never told me, I thought.

"Not having that conversation here," Hunter said calmly, looking back at me with a smile. "How are you feeling?" he asked, sitting down in the chair on the other side of the bed next to me.

I slowly nodded, pressing my lips into a thin line. "I feel fine," I said, looking back at Jagger. "I would like to go home. When can I leave?"

"That's the doc's call, sweet girl." Jagger leaned back, still holding my hand in his. The reassurance he gave me made me feel safe. Whenever he was close, I was safe. I knew it no matter what. And the same way I was starting to feel about Hunter. His presence alone was enough to make me feel warm and protected.

"I will call for him then." I reached up to the button to request a nurse or doctor. "I want to get out of here. I want to go back to work as soon as possible—" I stopped, my eyes widening. "Oh no, I've not told Frankie! He must be looking for me everywhere."

"He knows, Low. Don't worry," Jagger said, calming me just a bit.

"What did he say? Adeline won't be working this week because of her college exams," I said, afraid that she had to fill in for me on her off-days.

Jag interrupted me. "Frankie wants you to get better. He said he can find another girl to take over your shifts this week, so don't worry, all right? It's all good and he wishes you a speedy recovery."

I nodded slowly, making a mental note to call

him and thank him. I wanted to go back to work and college soon. Although, I wasn't taking school very seriously at the moment. Working and earning money was more important.

The door opened and Dr. Sullivan stood there, taking in the scene in front of him. "Why, what a wonderful surprise. Have you guys spent the night here in those chairs?" he joked, grinning from ear to ear and going straight to the end of my bed to look at the clipboard.

My gaze turned to Jagger, then Hunter, who was quickly looking away from Jagger. A small gleam of mischief crossed his eyes and I couldn't hold back a stupidly cheesy grin. Him staying longer than he was allowed wasn't exactly him staying all night, but it came close.

"Nah, just wanted to be here as early as possible," Jagger answered in an almost sarcastic tone. God, he just had to make me feel awkward.

"Well, I am glad you're up," Doc said, looking at me with a smile. "How are we feeling?"

"Good. Very good. I was hoping to go home soon."

"Very optimistic, aren't we?" His voice was cheerful and welcome as always, but I wasn't sure he was letting me go so quickly.

"I would like to check on the ribs and lungs and make sure they'll be fine without the help of the machine. That will take some hours." He looked up to Jagger and Hunter. "How about you two go get some real breakfast and come by after lunch, hmm? I'll know more after the exam but it's not really necessary for you to stay here and wait."

He wasn't really kicking them out but I wanted them to be productive today too. Waiting for me to get better wasn't gonna help either of us.

"I'll be fine. See you later," I said, looking at Hunter, then back at Jagger.

He nodded, standing up and kissing my forehead. "Love you," he whispered, then walked out of the room, probably knowing Hunter's goodbye wasn't something he needed to see.

Hunter got up from his chair, cupping my face with his hands and kissing my lips softly but determined. I smiled into the kiss, not wanting him to let go.

"See you later, love," he mumbled into the kiss, then his tongue came out to touch mine and just as quickly, his mouth was gone. I looked up at him, feeling the blood in my body run wild.

"Bye," I managed to say before he left the room with a wink and a charming smile.

"Most girls don't even get one guy to love them the way they love you. Cherish that," Dr. Sullivan said with a smile. I nodded slowly.

"Forever."

CHAPTER THIRTY-SEVEN

Hunter

Jagger told me to get into his car when we exited the hospital. I didn't respond. I just walked over to his car and got into the passenger's side. He was about to give me a talk I never even thought about. *A way out* was never my plan. But since Harlow, I was thinking about leaving my old life behind and starting over. Growing up, I always knew I wasn't going to be one of those kids who went to college or worked at some retail store or nine-to-five job. Well, I probably wasn't smart enough for college anyway. I wasn't book-smart. I was more of a street-smart kind of guy. I knew my way around the city, knew how to deal with difficult situations, and handle business in a way some nerdy college guy wouldn't be able to handle. I grew up that way and I wasn't giving it up. Ever since living at that orphanage, I grew stronger mentally. I didn't need a family to help me grow. All I needed was myself. Then I eventually grew up and met some people I knew were gonna help me get to where I was now. Jagger wasn't one of them since I was the one helping him get where he was right now.

He was working for a mechanic and fixed up my car multiple times when I first came to Hastings. I remember seeing his bloody noses and busted lips every time I brought my car in, and one day I asked him why he was always beaten up every time I saw him. He then told me about the underground fighting and how he earned some extra money from it. One day he told me to go see one of his fights and the next time I saw him I told him to stop that bullshit and come work for Gunner.

Now, Gunner was what uneducated, normal people would call a gang leader. A drug lord. But he was so much more than that. I met Gunner after living in Hastings for a month. I was selling my stuff in an alley where some of his guys already sold and when they first caught me there I thought they would start a fight. They were carrying guns, not bothered about others seeing them on their waistbands. After a quick talk, they told me I should either fuck off or go with them to see their boss. I wasn't even hesitant because I knew if I had someone giving me tasks to fulfill I'd bring in more money. So I went and those two guys introduced me to Gunner.

I knew I would be doing illegal shit with him as my boss, but I didn't think Hastings had more to offer than just drugs and guns. About ten other people, including Jagger, worked for Gunner at the moment, and we were doing our best to keep up with all the other gangs surrounding this city. Our business was growing, with more and more people reaching out to us and asking for help and support. Most of them wanted revenge for something a friend or family member had done and those people mostly offered huge amounts of money. We never turned down an offer. Not even when we had to take down people.

"Explain," Jagger simply said as he sat down next to me in his car. His expression was blank and he was waiting for me to talk. I sighed, leaning back in the seat and running my hands through my hair.

"She deserves to know the truth about me. I've treated her wrong for so long. I can't keep it up and have her next to me."

"So don't," he simply said, shrugging and raising an eyebrow. "You've dragged me into this and I will not allow you to just leave because you think you're in love with my sister. We're fucking partners, man. The shit we get assigned takes two most of the time and you know we get crazy money out of it. I just bailed out my fucking father with that money and I don't even feel bad because I know I still have enough to pay rent, food, and Low's college. I need this job and I can't do it without you."

Everything he said made perfect sense. I had too much money too, but using it for anything else than what was necessary to live wasn't a choice. We both grew up with no money and the town knows that. If we would suddenly buy a new house or new clothes, they would start to wonder where it all came from. And we didn't need anyone to interfere in our lives.

Yet, all he said wasn't really cutting it for me. Only one thing really stuck with me. "I don't think I love her. I know it."

Fuck me. I confessed my love for Harlow in front of her damn brother. And the look I got from him was telling me exactly how stupid I sounded. But shit, saying it out loud made my heart pound in my chest and I was so close to getting out of that car and running up to her room to tell her.

"Who the fuck are you?" he asked, his voice amused but still angry. I didn't know what to answer. Who was I? I had changed so quickly that not even I realized what was happening. I was turning into a lovesick man and I knew it would break her one day. But I couldn't let her go. Not now that I got her.

"I'm fucked up, I know that. And I know this job is all I ever wanted. But I'm not sure I can keep it from her. I feel like I can't hide from her anymore."

Jagger nodded slowly, looking down at the steering wheel. "We have to be at the cave at ten. We'll get a new task and I need you to cooperate, all right? I've been hiding all this from her for all this time and she knows I don't want her to ask about my nights out. She respects that but I know it's not right. She's all I got and the money I get out of it helps us both. But she knows I have a job working as a mechanic, and as long as I keep that up, she won't ask any more questions." He turned his gaze to me, studying me for a while. "You should probably get a normal job. You know, to cover."

A normal job. Jesus Christ.

CHAPTER THIRTY-EIGHT

Hunter

Jagger decided to get some burgers and fries for lunch, and since we had to wait on Harlow getting checked by the doc, we drove out to Harvey's Diner where Bliss worked. I was sure she was working today and I hadn't seen her in a while, so I thought going there wasn't such a bad idea.

As we entered the diner, Bliss's eyes were instantly on me, and a wide grin broke out on her face. If I hadn't grown up with her, I probably never would have wanted to have anything to do with her. She's obnoxious and loud for those who don't really know her, but she had a big heart. She was also a bitch, always wanting to be the best at everything. At least when she was younger. Now, this would sound rude and harsh since she's my sister, but the number of fights she got into as a teenage girl was incredible, and having our foster parents grounding her almost every weekend was record-breaking. We were once put into a home in Denver, Colorado, and people around town called her *Terror*. Of course, Bliss didn't mind being called that and she once told me her behaving the way she did was freeing and fun.

She was a grown-up woman now. Her wild behavior settled down a bit, and I was so fucking thankful for it. She was a pain in the ass most of the time, texting and calling me to tell me how awful I was at being a brother, not visiting her enough at work or her home.

"How much did you pay him to come here?" she asked Jagger, still grinning and walking around the counter to hug him first. Jagger let out a chuckle, hugging her back.

"Apparently enough," he answered, shoving his fists into his pockets. I shrugged, letting my sister kiss my cheek, then run her hand through my hair a bit too roughly.

"Damn, Hun. You still getting into fights?" Bliss said, pointing at my nose.

"Jesus, stop," I said, annoyed by her need to get on my nerves. "We just need some food and then we're out of here."

Bliss laughed, rolling her eyes and nodding toward a table by the window. "Sit. Burgers, fries and Coke?" she asked, raising her brows. Jagger and I both nodded, then took a seat at the booth.

"She still with that douche from Kearney?" Jagger asked, leaning back and rolling up the sleeves of his flannel. I shook my head. "Think she broke it off. Last time she complained about driving to Kearny every weekend for an hour to find him drunk at a bar."

He nodded slowly, taking out his phone and putting it on the table. "She deserves better. I mean, she is a handful, but she's got some brain."

I knew he wasn't trying to hit on her. Jagger was too good for a girl like Bliss. He needed someone calm and stable, not mentally crazed and incredibly talkative. Jagger was a good guy. Well, besides the shit he did at work. He was caring. Just the way he treated Low was fascinating, but then I wasn't sure he could love any other girl more than sweet Harlow. She was his everything.

"If you ever find a man strong enough to handle her physically and mentally, let me know," I joked.

Jagger's phone lit up and his eyes immediately went to the screen, reading what was written on the message.

"Everything okay?" I asked, knowing he was waiting on an update on Harlow.

"It's Low. It'll take some hours." He turned and pushed his phone over to my side of the table to let me read her text.

Doc said he needs an MRI. It will take a while. I'll text you as soon we're done here. Love you x – Low

I read the text twice before giving him back his phone and nodded. "Let's relax a little. She'll be okay." Jagger typed a quick reply, then nodded and leaned back again.

"Here you go." Bliss put two plates down in front of us and filled up our glasses with Coke. "Anything new? Something I should know? Any stories you wanna tell me?"

I rolled my eyes, taking a sip from my drink and then shaking my head. "Don't you have work to do?" I asked, annoyed. She shrugged, then looked over at Jagger with a smile. "So?"

"He thinks he's in love with my sister," Jagger said in an almost ironic tone.

Even though I wasn't up for this conversation, I couldn't help it. "I know I am." Great.

"Huh?" Bliss's surprised voice made me look at her, and her facial expression was confused. "Wait, you have a sister?"

Jagger nodded, quickly looking at me before returning Bliss's gaze. "Wow, we've known each other for a while, yet you don't know that I have a sister."

"Guess we never really talked. What's her name?" Bliss asked, now grinning again. I started eating because I knew where this was going. Fuck me.

"Low. Well, Harlow. No fucking clue what she sees in him, but I guess I can't just tell her not to date him. She's almost twenty."

Bliss didn't respond to that and I was scared as hell to look up at her. I knew she was giving me a death-stare. After a few moments of silence, I looked up at her, her hands on her hips, her lips puckered up, and one of her brows shot up. She remembered Harlow.

"I've met her before," she said slowly, turning her gaze back at Jagger. "She's a real sweetheart. How's she doing?" Bliss was pissed, to say the least. She'd seen me mistreat her the last time we came here and she was the one who drove her home. I followed her car, making sure Harlow would get home safe, and I parked a few houses down from hers, just observing her from inside my car like a fucking creep.

Jagger eyed me for a while before looking back up at my sister. "She's at the hospital. Got run over by a car two nights ago. Broken ribs and collapsed lung, but she's strong and going to be all right."

Bliss's hand shot up to cover her mouth and her eyes widened. "Oh my God!" Her other hand reached out to Jagger and touched his shoulder. "I'm so sorry," she said, tears appearing in her eyes. Jagger shrugged, looking back at me, then taking some fries into his mouth. "She's incredibly strong-willed and she's already doing so much better."

Way to make me feel even worse. My heart ached and I wanted to turn back time and undo everything that happened.

Bliss sighed, letting her hand fall from her mouth, then smiled at Jagger with a genuine, sad smile. "I'd like to visit her if that's okay."

"We'll go by later. She's just getting tested and all that, but you're welcome to come with us."

I didn't mind her coming. Harlow told me she liked Bliss the day we came here. They were nice to each other and I thought both of them could use a female friend to talk to.

But I also had lots of explaining to do.

CHAPTER THIRTY-NINE

Hunter

Bliss finally left our table, letting us eat our food without her constant questioning. I had shit coming my way now that she knew who Harlow was and what had happened to her. Bliss somehow new Jagger didn't tell her the whole truth and what had led to Low being hit by a car. I knew she was going to ask me about it, and why I now suddenly was in love with her when just a few days earlier I had acted like an asshole outside the diner.

Bliss was confused as to how I could've fallen in love with Harlow so quickly. I thought about that last night and the only thing that came to mind was the panic and fear of not having her anymore. Before the accident, I hadn't realized what kind of woman Harlow was—one I would want to keep close—but instead, I treated her badly. Now, knowing that anything could happen to her and I could lose her was scaring the shit out of me. I never realized how much of an impact one person

171

could have if I just let them in for once, instead of playing with their feelings and messing with their minds.

All that sounded so wrong in my mind. I wasn't that type of guy, and conflicted didn't sound right. I was more than conflicted. I was in deep misery, and even if my brain was telling me to go back to being an asshole, my heart was ripping itself apart with the thought of losing Harlow. She was giving me a chance to show her who I was and messing up once more wasn't really on my list.

Once again, the word confused didn't even come close to the way I really felt. My thoughts were running wild. Fuck me.

"Jesus, man," Jagger mumbled, raising an eyebrow at me. "Stop overthinking everything and concentrate. We got some stuff to handle tonight and I need you to cope."

"How can you act like nothing's happened? It's your sister I want, you do realize that, right?" I asked, trying to find some clearance about that for myself. Christ, I was about to go mental. All of this was messing with me.

"I got that," he simply said and then shrugged. "And she wants you too. I've warned you before, and another beating is already on my list of things I would do to you if you break her heart, but I'm not going to push myself between the two of you. I hate the thought of you and my sister together. You've been my brother for so damn long. But if it's what makes her happy, I won't interfere. Your business. Now, I don't want to hear any more of that. I'm done talking about it and I just want to do my job and keep living the way I did before this all happened. I know it's messing with your mind. Mine too, man. But we gotta push it aside now."

I was trying to figure out if he was being honest about that or just trying to tempt me to mess up, but his eyes at that moment were just as expressive as his sister's and I knew he was being very sincere. If that's how he felt about all of it, I was sure I could settle my thoughts a bit.

I slowly nodded. "Thanks."

He gave me a half-smile, taking the last bite of his burger and then leaning, propping his arm over the back of the booth. He grabbed his phone and looked down at the screen with a frown. He got up and held his phone to his ear. "Be right back," he said before leaving the booth and going outside. Probably not about Harlow, or he would've told me. I knew he still had some shit to handle because of his father. If he wanted to talk about it, he knew I would listen.

"Wanna tell me what the fuck has gotten into you, Hun?" Bliss's voice was like an alarm going off early in the morning. Annoying as hell.

She sat down in the booth where Jagger had sat and propped up her elbows on the table and her chin on her hands. I sighed, ran my hand through my hair, and shook my head. "Not really sure, sis."

"You hurt her that night and went ape-shit on her. I had to drive her home while she was crying and then you had the audacity to sit in your car outside her house, observing her like a creep. And now you wanna tell me that you fell in love with her?"

"Fuck, Bliss. Wanna call the local radio station so the people who aren't in here can hear about that too?" I asked sarcastically, pointing out the people around us now eyeing me.

"Go on," she pushed, tilting her head to the side.

I took a deep breath, not really wanting to explain anything to her. She would find out, though. So what's the point?

"She came to visit me at the T.P. but changed her mind and ran off, then got hit by a car. Before that, I had told her not to come to see me there, but she didn't listen. I'm not saying it's her fault. I didn't answer her calls and messages. We talked and we're figuring things out. I've put her through some shit and she knows I wanna make it better."

"And you really think you can be a guy she deserves?" she asked, almost amused with what she was saying. I shrugged.

"I'm trying my best, all right? I wanna try to be good. For her. And maybe also for myself."

"Hunter," she sighed, shaking her head. "How on earth are you going to be any good for her or yourself when you never got any help?"

I knew what she was talking about, but I've been through that once and it didn't help. "I can try. I don't need any docs or therapists to help me."

"And you actually think you will be able to change from one day to another without any help? You raged out there last time you were here and she cried. How many times have you been aggressive in her presence?" She was keeping her voice low, but she wasn't holding back on the anger.

"I said I will try!" She was triggering me and she

knew exactly how to get to me. I was slowly starting to explode. Each time this happened, my body started to shake from the inside and my muscles tensed.

"You're sick, Hunter. Have you told her that?" she asked, gritting her teeth. Her eyes turned dark and I knew she was just trying to help me.

I was doing my best to keep it inside. Going off at my sister was never a good idea. She knew exactly how to handle me and I was not going to give in so easily.

"I'm not sick." I felt my eyes tear up. Hearing it from her only made me realize how right she was.

Bliss bit her bottom lip, shaking her head slowly and reaching out to grab my hand. She squeezed it tightly.

"Being bipolar should be taken seriously, Hun. And you know how serious I am about it. I've always wanted you to get better. Help you handle it all, but you always refused. You know I'm here, and I think this time it would be best if you would listen to me. For once."

CHAPTER FORTY

Hunter

"Damn, Bliss," Jagger said, now standing next to the booth, looking down at us. "How on earth did you make this fucker cry?" His tone was mocking, and I quickly brushed away the one tear rolling down my face. I hadn't cried in a while. Not sure when the last time was that I did, but it was long ago. I never wanted to face this. I pushed it aside and hoped no one would get to me the way Bliss did right now. I didn't allow people to get that close and thank fuck they didn't.

Growing up in different homes with different parents and spending years and years trying to figure out why my mom and dad left me at the orphanage when I was a baby was a memory I wanted to make disappear. I hated thinking about it and it only made me angrier. I'd met Bliss at the orphanage. We were both still little and were one day put into a home together at which we stayed for almost a year. The foster parents we had weren't really qualified to foster orphan kids, but no one ever did a really good background check on them. The people we lived with were in their thirties and only one of them worked. They didn't have a lot of money, and even if I was only four, I knew something was wrong with them. There was smoke in the air in every room of the house and the furniture was old and dirty. We didn't have many toys to play with. Just one small soccer ball, a puzzle, and a hairless Barbie. I remember thinking I finally had a mom and dad I could spend the rest of my life with, but I was so damn wrong. Those people didn't care for us or our health. They never really cooked, instead ordered pizza or Chinese food every day. All they cared about was the money they got from the city, which was meant to be used for us, Bliss and me. For new clothes, healthy food, and books and toys. We got none of that. Six-year-old Bliss told me made-up stories each night so I could fall asleep. Most of them were about two kids with superpowers, saving the world from evil people who took orphan kids into their homes and treated them poorly. Unlike our reality, those super-kids always won and lived happily ever after.

The real trauma started on my birthday. I turned five that day and I was excited, jumping up and down on the bed I shared with Bliss because the people who took us in promised me a Superman cake and a new Superman figure. The funny thing was, I was naïve enough to believe after months of playing with just three things and eating the same shit over and over again, they would suddenly come home with a big cake and a new toy.

Of course, they didn't do any of that. It was early in the morning and I had woken up with the sun and a big smile on my face. I woke up Bliss, telling her how excited I was, and she sang happy birthday to me. I couldn't sit still that morning and I broke one of the few rules we had to follow in that house: *Don't come out of the bedroom until the alarm goes off.*

The alarm clock sat on the bedside table and it was set to ring at ten-thirty every morning. Up until that time, Bliss and I were both starving from not eating enough the evening before and having to wait until lunch to come. We got used to it eventually.

It was my birthday, so I thought that that one rule could be broken once. But I was so horribly wrong, and knocking on the bedroom door of those people who made our life a living hell was the worst mistake I had ever made.

"I guess it's just a sister-thing," Bliss said quietly, noticing me not being really present. I blinked multiple times, thankful for her interruption. My thoughts were about to go somewhere dark and I couldn't handle that at the moment.

"I'm done with my shift. I'll get changed, and then I wanna go visit Harlow with you two." Bliss got up from her seat and patted my shoulder. She bent down, kissing my temple softly.

When she left, Jagger sat back down and studied my face for a moment. "You okay?"

I nodded, looking up at him with a tight smile. "Just some past shit. Nothing to worry about." Jagger knew a lot about me, just like I knew a lot about him. But this I kept secret. Bliss was the only person who I knew could handle all of this, and I didn't want anyone else to feel the need to help me out with my problems. I didn't want to bother anyone with it.

"I'm here, all right?" Jagger said in a lower voice. I nodded again, knowing he was not just saying that to make me feel better. "Yeah, me too."

Bliss came back and we headed out to Jagger's car. The drive to the hospital was silent, and I thought about waiting to go there since the doc and Harlow said they would inform us when she was done. I didn't want to rush her, but I needed to see her again. Luckily, just as we pulled up to the parking lot in front of the hospital, Jagger received a text from Harlow, saying she was done with all the examinations. Thank fuck.

We went up to her room and Jagger knocked, going in first, then I followed him and Bliss was close behind me. I saw Harlow smile as soon as she saw her brother, and just that made me want to pull her into my arms and keep her as close as possible. She was full of joy and I was still surprised by how well she was doing after the accident. Talk about superpowers.

"I brought someone who wanted to see you. I hope you don't mind," Jagger said, kissing Harlow's forehead and then looking back at Bliss. Harlow's eyes went directly to Bliss and her smile grew. "Bliss, so nice to see you."

"You too, darling. How are you feeling?" Bliss asked. I shoved my fists in my pocket, a little hurt about the fact that she hadn't even looked at me yet. "I feel better. Much better." Harlow's eyes went back to Jagger, then finally, they traveled over to me and her smile faded while her eyes grew slightly bigger and fear mixed with empathy danced around her gaze.

"Have you been crying?" she asked softly, holding out her hand to me and, damn...I guess she could read me just as well as I read her.

CHAPTER FORTY-ONE

Hunter

I walked over to her, taking her hand in mine and lifting it to my lips to kiss it softly while looking into her eyes. "I'm all good, sweetheart," I assured her. But she was already on to me, and the look she gave me told me she didn't believe one bit of those words.

"Are you sure?" she asked, lifting an eyebrow and squeezing my hand slightly. My lips pressed into a thin line and I lowered my head, kissing her cheek.

"Not here," I whispered in her ear, letting her know I wasn't going to talk about it with my sister and her brother in the room. If I was going to tell her everything about my messed up brain, I wanted to do it with only her in my presence. Harlow nodded, a worried look coming over her face. I gave her a small smile, hoping she could be patient enough to wait until we were alone.

"What did the doc say?" Jagger asked, pretty

181

much helping me out. Or he was just hoping to change the subject because I knew it was still a bit weird for him to see us getting this close. I let go of her hand and took a step back, then sat down in the chair by the window on the other side of the room. I rubbed the stubbles on my jaw, taking in the scene in front of me. It was strange seeing my sister, my best friend, and Harlow at once. I've always wanted to keep them separated from each other because each of them handled me differently. Bliss was blunt with her words and thoughts. She never kept anything hidden from me and always checked in as soon as she knew something was going on. Jagger was not only my best friend but also my partner. The things we did weren't something for weak-hearted people and we also had to keep most of our business to ourselves. Of course, other guys we worked with knew about the things we did. But I shouldn't have told Bliss about any of the jobs we'd done. I should've kept it secret, just like Jagger did with Harlow. But Bliss wasn't Harlow. My sister took it hard at first, shouted at me, and even threatened me. She was fucking pissed the day she made me tell her where I got the money from that I had used to get her a new apartment. At first, I was trying to keep it to myself, and not telling her sounded better than letting her in on the shit I did to earn money, but when Bliss wanted to know something, she wouldn't back down until she knew. So my only way out of her screaming my ears off was to tell her.

She was handling it better now, knowing I wasn't going to get hurt. I was good with guns and knives. They didn't scare me, and handling one of those weapons made me feel strong. I had power over everything for once. Growing up the way I did was hard, and power wasn't something I had felt until the first night working for Gunner. He offered me a job that would get me two thousand dollars, and that amount of money was a lot for just setting up a small car bomb and making sure the guy driving it would die the second he turned on the engine. It was easy money, and indirectly killing someone gave me a huge adrenalin thrust. I wanted more. And I also realized it was the only thing I was good at. So why would I ever stop?

"I'm not allowed to go home yet. I don't need help breathing but my lungs are still aching a bit." Harlow's voice broke through my thoughts and I looked back up to Harlow from the plant sitting in a corner I was blankly staring at. Damn, she looked beautiful in a messy ponytail and natural face.

"I can't really walk. My ribs are still healing and standing up is a bit hard."

"Staying here for a while is probably the best idea, " Jagger said with the same worried expression she gave me just minutes ago.

"You're right." Her voice was calm, still, you could tell she was slightly annoyed that she wasn't allowed to go home. "I would like to take a shower."

"Okay." Jagger gave her a small smile, looking over to the bathroom door.

"I don't have fresh clothes here. Or my towel," Harlow added.

"We'll get that for you, sweet girl." Jagger

looked over to Bliss, nodding toward the door. "Let's go back home to get her things. You probably know best what she needs." Bliss quickly nodded, smiling at Harlow, and then looking over to me. They were going to give us some space. Perfect.

As soon as they left, I turned my gaze to Harlow, her eyes already fixed on me. We stayed quiet for a while, then she inhaled deeply and let the air out of her body again. "I don't like seeing you like this."

The corner of my mouth lifted slightly and I ran my hand over my face. "There's just a lot on my mind," I told her, looking back up at her.

She nodded slowly. "Will you talk to me about it?" she asked and I nodded quickly.

"One step at a time, remember, love?" I said with a small smile, then standing up and walking over to her. "I know. It's just…" She sighed, her brows narrowing. "I know something's going on, but I just don't know how to help you if you don't communicate with me."

My hands cupped her face, running my thumbs over her soft cheeks. "I need to figure some things out, make sure everything fits into place, and I promise I will tell you everything after."

"Hunter…"

"Hey, listen to me," I said in a lower voice, almost whispering. I bent down so we were eye to eye. "I told you I need to figure things out, and as soon as I do, you can ask me anything. But for now, let me tell you what I choose to tell you. Is that good enough?"

She was hesitant, making me wait on her

response. She studied my face, letting her eyes travel all over my face until they stopped at my lips.

"Kiss me," she whispered. I smiled now, pressing my lips to hers and taking in her sweet taste.

Chapter Forty-Two

Harlow

His lips moving against mine and his tongue dancing with mine made me feel better. It was a stupid thing to say, but his kiss was more useful than any medicine Dr. Sullivan had given me in the past few days. I felt better, knowing Hunter wasn't leaving. Although, him coming in here with teary eyes made me worry about him. Even more than before. I knew something was going on. Something he was holding back, and it probably wasn't something I would accept, or else he would've told me before. But just like with Jagger, I wasn't going to stick my nose into their business unless they were open to telling me themselves.

Of course, nothing good was going on with them. Jagger never talked to me about it, but I knew drugs were involved. He even carried a gun with him most days and that gun wasn't to protect him or me from the people in Hastings. We were safe enough as long as we kept our mouths shut and went on with our lives as if nothing ever happened. At least for me, nothing ever happened.

I decided that letting him move at his own pace was best for both of us. I didn't want to rush things or put him in a situation where he would just get mad because I'd pushed him into telling me all his secrets. There were things I wasn't supposed to know and he didn't have to tell me anything he felt uncomfortable with. For now, this was okay. One step at a time, just like he said.

His tongue pushed into my mouth while his fingers made their way into my hair at the back of my head. A small moan escaped me as he fisted his hands, pulling at the roots of my hair and loosening up my ponytail a bit. God, how I missed this. Our kiss turned quickly into a passionate make-out and I was happy Jagger and Bliss had left the room. I lifted my hands, one touching his chest, grabbing his sweatshirt tightly, and the other holding onto the side of his neck. Luckily, I was sitting, because I knew my knees would've given out by now.

His kiss was consuming me slowly and it almost felt like he was trying to tell me something. His lips and tongue moved passionately against mine, and his hands started to pull a little more at my hair, then pushing my face against him a bit more so he could dive deeper into the kiss. He had never kissed me like this before. He was so determined, yet tender.

I let him lead me, wondering if he had the intention to stop sooner or later. Either way, I didn't mind sitting here, making out with Hunter like two teenagers.

"We should probably stop," Hunter murmured under his breath, but instead of letting go, he pressed his lips against mine again. I smiled then, thinking it was too funny that he couldn't resist.

I let out a chuckle, pushing against his chest with one hand. "Then stop," I challenged, my own words making me grin. Now he was the one chuckling and one of his hands cupped the back of my head, gripping at my ponytail.

"I can't wait to have you to myself again." His lips left mine and our eyes locked. We were both out of breath and I suddenly felt empty without his lips touching mine. "But I guess your brother wants to spend some time with you too after you get out of here."

I nodded slowly, smiling softly. "I want that too," I told him, looking down at his lips. "But when I'm allowed to go home, the first thing I want to do is cuddle on the couch and watch a movie with all of you."

Hunter studied my face for a while, licking his lips before nodding and giving me one last kiss. "Anything you want, love."

Almost half an hour passed as Jagger opened the door after knocking and Bliss followed right behind. A nurse came in last, pushing a little cart with bandages and what looked like plastic wrap on it. "So, you're ready to take a shower?" she asked with a smile, and I nodded quickly, letting Hunter step away from me. I felt Jagger's eyes on me before they went to Hunter, who shoved his fists into his pockets and stood there looking a bit unsure about what to say or do. Usually, Hunter was the one who stood there with his head up high, full of confidence that scared me in the beginning.

"I will help you shower. If your ribcage hurts too much, we can just put some plastic around your bandage. But if you want to change it, we can do that too."

"I'd like to take this bandage off to shower. I think I'll handle without it for a few minutes."

The nurse nodded and walked over to my side. She looked up, obviously a little overwhelmed with all the people standing there and watching her. "You guys should wait outside," I told them and smiled to assure them I was fine.

Jagger didn't respond at first. God, this was slightly awkward. "Take care of her," Hunter said to the nurse and I rolled my eyes. The nurse knew what she was doing and I was sure it wasn't the first time she helped a patient take a shower. It was her job. Hunter seemed a little jealous, which made this whole situation even worse.

"Let's get some snacks," Bliss suggested and put the duffle bag with my things in it on the bed. "I'll get you some chocolate. It will make you better." I returned her smile and waited until the three of them left the room, with Hunter scowling at the nurse one last time.

"They seem very protective," the nurse said with a smile. I looked up at her and nodded. "They are. Sometimes it's a little too much, believe it or not."

She shrugged and helped me sitting up at the side of the bed. "Some get a lot, and some get none." I knew what she meant by that. I had to appreciate what I had. I did, but the nurse didn't

189

know about our past. We had a whole different dynamic, which was scary at times.

CHAPTER FORTY-THREE

Hunter

Leaving the hospital took almost three weeks for Harlow and watching a movie right after she got out didn't go as she had imagined. Only fifteen minutes into the movie she fell asleep with her head in my lap and a small blanket over her body. She wasn't as fit as she thought she was before we got here and it made me grin when I realized her breathing had evened out and her mind was now in a state of dreaming. Too damn adorable.

I brushed back her hair, looking down at her beautiful face, and then glancing over at Jagger, who was sitting in the recliner, his elbows propped on his knees and his hands rubbing against each other, almost in a nervous gesture. He met my gaze, lifting an eyebrow and nodding toward Harlow.

"Should've known she would pass out sooner or later. She looked tired as hell," he said in a slightly lower voice, so as not to wake his sister up. I nodded.

"I'll put her to bed." I lifted her head slowly, making sure she wouldn't wake up, and after getting up myself, I picked Harlow up in my arms and walked her to her room. When she was lying in her bed, I covered her up and made sure she was comfortable. She had told me her ribs didn't hurt thanks to her painkillers, but I still didn't want to make her uncomfortable.

Bending down, I kissed the corner of her mouth softly and then whispered, "Sleep tight, my love."

"Well, I guess I won't be needed anymore," Bliss said as I got back to the living room. She was already standing, smiling at me softly. "If you need me, let me know."

"Yeah," Jagger said, looking up to my sister. "You could come back around nine-thirty. We gotta go to the cave and I don't want Low to be home alone for now. Maybe bring some food. Have some girl-talk or whatever."

Bliss studied first Jagger, then me. Then she sighed. "You two better be careful. I think to lose you would hurt her more than anything."

Not sure who that was directed to, but I think Jagger and I both felt it. I nodded and put my arm around her to hug her goodbye. "We got this," I assured her.

Bliss frowned, looking up at me. "Still a dangerous job you do. Even if you're good at it," she whispered.

I nodded again, then gave her a cocky grin. "We're the best at it."

Jagger chuckled in agreement, now leaning back in the recliner and spreading his knees to make it more comfortable.

"Of course you are." With that, she gave us a quick wave and then headed out of the front door.

When it closed behind her, I sat back down on the couch and leaned back, taking in a deep breath. "What kind of job do you think it is this time?" I asked in a low voice. Even if I had closed the door to Harlow's bedroom, I wanted to make sure she wouldn't hear us talking about this. I didn't want her to find out about this. Not this way, that is.

"I'd be up for a killing assignment," he said bluntly. "Still got some anger in me because of you I would like to get out. Don't think you would be able to handle another one of my beatings." Now he was smirking, almost challenging me.

I laughed, shaking my head. "To be honest, man, I don't think so either." Truth was, Jagger was a great fighter. And if I didn't come along that time at the underground boxing ring, seeing him kick some ass, I think he would've become a real MMA fighter. But fighting on a real stage was mostly just for show. Starting drama with people you didn't even know and making them bleed and break their bones. What Jagger did was easy money. But this, working for Gunner, was even easier. And it was nice knowing somebody had your back.

Jagger's phone rang and he quickly looked at the screen. His face immediately turned serious and he kept on holding the phone in his hand, not answering it.

"Not gonna get that?" I asked, trying to figure out who could possibly be calling him. Gunner never called. Texts were his only way of communicating with us when we weren't standing directly in front of him.

"Nah," he simply said. The phone had stopped ringing and Jagger's tense shoulders relaxed again.

"Everything okay, man?" I asked. He nodded once, putting down the phone on the coffee table in front of us. He propped up his elbows on his knees again, leaning forward and rubbing his face with both his hands.

I gave him a minute, not wanting to push him to tell me who it was. Then, his phone started to ring again and we both looked down at the screen immediately.

Dean was written on it, and I lifted my gaze to Jagger's face. He looked like he was about to explode or punch something. I knew Dean was his and Harlow's father, and I also knew they just bailed him out of jail. I knew a lot about Dean and his behavior by the way he treated his young children.

"I thought you told him not to contact you."

"I did." He grabbed his phone, staring at the screen. "Ungrateful piece of shit," Jagger murmured before touching his thumb to the screen and then lifting his phone to his ear. I took a glance over at the hallway, to make sure Harlow wouldn't come out at this very moment.

"The fuck do you need, Dean."

I didn't hear any of what his father was saying on the other side of the line, but I bet it was fucking entertaining. From what Jagger told me, Dean was a dirty, manipulative bastard. Not a father anyone needed. Lucky I didn't have one. Better off with no

194

father than one like Dean, I thought.

As Jagger listened to his father talk, I leaned back and waited for this call to be over. His eyes traveled up to mine, then he shook his head and gave me an annoyed look.

Well, that could end in any possible situation.

CHAPTER FORTY-FOUR

Jagger

Dean wasn't a person I needed in my life. Not since the day I finally had taken enough of his bullshit and packed up the few things we got and left him behind. But that day the cops called, telling me that he drunk drove on the highway like a crazed man and harassed people at several gas stations around Grand Island, I knew I had some shit coming my way. Some major shit.

He was always bad news. What Low didn't know was that wasn't the first time I had to bail Dean out. It was the third, and hopefully the last time I had to go and get him. Sweet Low didn't need to know that, though. And the last two times I got him out of jail, I hadn't seen or spoken to him. I just went to the police station, paid the amount of money that was needed to let him run free again, and left without a word. Not sure he even knew I was the one paying. Although, I was sure he had lost every friend he has ever had in the past. The last time, though, I had enough of his fucking childish and toxic behavior. Dean was a master manipulator. Lucky, me and Harlow didn't get any of that from his DNA. Sometimes I wondered if he even was our father, but that day we saw him at the police station, his resemblance to my reflection in the mirror was proof enough that I was his blood. We had the same mouth, nose, and jawline, only things different were his wrinkles.

I had enough going on in my life working for Gunner and keeping up with everything that Low had to go through. She wasn't really doing well in college, missing many classes and not really studying for any of them. She'd much rather work at Frankie's, helping me paying off bills I already covered with my own money. I didn't want her to pay for anything. Not bills, not her college, not food. But I had to make her believe she was helping me out. Her heart was bigger than anyone's I'd ever met in my life, and telling her about my job would crush her, finding out I never really needed her help financially. Somehow it felt wrong keeping it all from her, but it all started the day she got the job at the diner and she was so damn happy after her first paycheck came in, beaming at me like a little girl getting candy, telling me she was finally making her wish come true to help me pay rent and food.

Instead of telling her I had enough money to buy a whole damn house, new furniture and probably also a new car, I hid all the money she gave me behind a loose tile in the bathroom. When I was ready to tell her, or if anything ever changed in our lives, I would get that money out and give it back to her.

Spending the money I had at the moment was not clever. Hastings wasn't rich. People around here worked their asses off to have a house and afford a normal living. For me, or even Hunter, that wasn't our goal. Not in Hastings. We both knew that if we suddenly drove around in a new car, we'd look suspicious and didn't want anyone to know about our job. We loved that job, even if it meant killing people we didn't know.

I knew it was wrong. Low could afford new clothes with that money, buy things she always wanted to have, but I was keeping it secret, hoping one day I could explain it all to her. I hated lying to her.

She was my all. The most precious thing in my damn life. And the thought of me breaking her heart in an almost deceitful way was killing me inside.

But for now, I had other things to deal with.

One thing was my father, the other my best friend. My best friend was turning into a whole other person. Fuck, it was strange seeing the two of them getting closer and knowing both of them were serious about it. At first, I thought Hunter would only want to experiment with her. He knew she was untouched and he probably saw her as a challenge. But the way he looked at her, and the way she let him get close without any fear in her eyes was proof enough for me. I had to let my protectiveness go and let my baby sister grow up. In the end, I couldn't keep her locked up and hidden from every man who wanted to get close. I just had to accept the idea that my best friend would be that man.

No, the other thing was way worse. Of course, worse in a whole different way. I knew Dean had my number, but I didn't know he had the guts to call me. Takes a lot of grit to call up a son who was beaten almost to death at one point as a kid. Not sure how he even dared to think about getting in contact with me, but here we were.

Hearing his voice made me tense up and feel sick at the same time. Knowing nothing good would come from this conversation, I braced myself and listened to his voice on the other side of the line.

"What's that language, son?" He chuckled, then I heard him take a pull from something, probably a cigarette. Damn, I needed one too. I looked over at Hunter, still sitting on the couch and watching me, his eyebrows slightly drawn together. He was worried. Not a surprise. We cared about each other and Dean was the center of some of our deep conversations. He knew about him, heard multiple stories about my past and what he did to Harlow and me.

I shook my head, letting him know I was pretty much done with this conversation already. Dean was a pain in the ass.

"Why did you call?" I asked, looking down at the coffee table. My voice was monotonous, letting him know I wasn't up for any of his shit.

He chuckled again, almost sounding drunk. To confirm my theory, three hard swallows and a small *pop* sound from his lips let me know he was drinking a beer. This could only get worse from here.

"Wanted to check in with my son. And how's

my daughter doing? That little ignorant bitch." The last words were slurred and I felt my blood boil.

"Relax," Hunter said in a low voice, making me realize I'd fisted my other hand and my veins ached at my neck. I looked up at him, trying to stay calm, not to wake up Low.

"I'll make sure you won't call me again. Don't try to come close, Dean. This is my final warning."

With that, I hung up on him, letting my phone drop on the recliner next to me. I ran my hands through my hair, gripping it tightly and pulling on the ends.

"It's all good, man. He won't get to you or Harlow. If he steps in Hastings territory, I'll handle him."

"I just wish he would fucking disappear from this earth." I got up, walking over to the fridge and taking out a beer. Unlike Dean, I drank beer to relax my body from people like him. I took two bottles out, opened them, and brought one over to Hunter. He took it, holding it in his hand and looking up at me while I drank some.

"Don't let him get to you." Hunter's words would most times calm me down automatically, letting me know he would always have my back. I nodded as a response, then sat back down.

"Just hoping he won't surprise Low at the diner. Don't think she could handle him on her own," I told him.

"We'll let Frankie know about Dean." Great idea. Why don't we let every single person in the city know about my fucking dad?

I knew Hunter was only trying to help me out,

and I appreciated it, but I started to wonder what it would be like to go against Dean on my own, making sure he would never even think about his oh so beloved kids again.

Or not being able to think at all.

Chapter Forty-Five

Harlow

I woke up to laughter and a moon shining right in my face. Despite all the rain in Hastings, when the sky cleared, the moon made sure to be seen. It didn't happen often and I always liked watching it up there and just get lost in my thoughts while staring at it. But when I opened my eyes and heard their voices in the living room, I was more interested in knowing what made them laugh out loud than the moon.

I must've fallen asleep watching the movie and someone put me to bed, which was nice. Though, I had other plans that afternoon. I wanted to be awake and close to my brother and Hunter. Bliss too, of course. Instead, I felt the effect the painkillers had on my body. I was weak but I had no pain. Lucky me.

I slowly sat up, putting one hand on my chest, feeling a bit weird because of my lungs. Breathing was okay, but I realized that taking small instead of deep breaths was more pleasant. Other than that funny feeling I had, everything was okay. So I got up, slow and steady, took the few steps to the door and opened it, walking down the hallway toward their laughter.

The second I turned the corner, I saw Jagger and Hunter sitting on the couch with their backs turned to me, and Bliss sitting on the recliner and gesturing wildly with her arms while talking. She was so preoccupied with telling a story that she didn't notice me standing there. I saw that as a great opportunity to just stand still and listen.

"I tried to warn him. I mean we all know what a sassy bitch I can be but he didn't listen. So my cocktail went straight down his crotch," Bliss said, shrugging and grinning. Jagger and Hunter both shook their heads and chuckled.

"I can't believe he actually tried to hit on you," Hunter said, amused. "You should've told me."

"Yeah, we could've stopped him," Jagger added, then leaned back. Bliss shrugged again, letting out a small laugh. "It was fun. Besides, I don't even think a man like Gunner could handle me."

Hunter laughed, nodding to approve of what his sister just said. "You're right, he couldn't."

Somehow, I felt like that was my cue to say something. "Who's Gunner?" My voice was quiet and hoarse. Perfect, now my vocal cords were giving in.

All three of them immediately turned their heads and locked eyes with me. At first, I thought none of them were going to say anything, and that I shouldn't have snuck up on them the way I did, but then Hunter snapped out of his little trance first, got up, and walked over to me, grabbing my face into his hands and eyeing me as if I was something he had never seen before. "Are you okay? You shouldn't have gotten up without help. You're weak. How are your ribs?" he said without taking a break between his words.

I narrowed my brows, grabbing both his shoulders to keep him calm. "I'm feeling better," I told him, hoping he would stop looking at me like a lost, confused pup who was searching for an answer in my face. When did he get so worried?

"Christ, Hunter. Let that girl breathe," Bliss said from behind him. I was still returning Hunter's gaze while I lightly squeezed his shoulders to signal I was okay. I really was.

"I feel better," I whispered so only he could hear and his eyes started to look less concerned.

Hunter nodded once, letting his eyes travel over my whole body before pressing his lips to mine. The kiss was short and I was glad he took a step back since my brother was right there in the room. I didn't want to make things any more awkward.

"Sleep well?" he asked with a small smile and I nodded as a response. Hunter realized that I was trying to distance him from myself, so he took a step to the side but put his hand on my lower back, almost as if he was trying to support me. Sweet of him, but something was bothering me about that situation.

I looked over at Jagger, pressing my lips into a thin line, and even if I was waiting on a response to my question, I asked again. "Who's Gunner?"

I had never really heard of any other guy Jagger knew and I never asked about any of them. I kept myself out of his business because he asked me to but something was off and I felt strange hearing from him.

"He's just a guy we're friendly with," Bliss said calmly, probably saving the other two from spilling anything I shouldn't know. I took a glance at Bliss before settling my eyes back on Jagger. I could tell he was on the verge of telling me something he'd kept to himself for a long time and that Gunner guy had triggered it. This was getting interesting.

But instead of telling me about it, Jagger got up and walked over to me with a small smile on his face. I felt Hunter move away to give us some space and I looked up at my brother. "I'm glad you're feeling better. Hunter and I need to be somewhere in thirty minutes and I'm not sure when I will be back tonight. Bliss brought some food. You two can have a little girl's night and watch some movies and talk."

I wanted to respond, but Jagger used his talking skills to not make any room for my words. "Love you," he added, kissing my head, then nodded to Hunter and walked out of the house without another word. Something was bothering him, and if I had the strength to, I would've run after him and not let him leave without talking to me. But he had things to do and I wasn't going to stand in his way. We could talk when he got back.

I looked over at Hunter, who was rubbing the back of his neck while looking at me a little confused. He was unsure about what to say, and for the first time, I wondered what could make Hunter Kane speechless.

I took a quick look at Bliss, because in all honesty; I was a bit confused and uncertain myself.

"Uh, I'll see you later," Hunter said, giving Bliss a quick look before heading out the door too.

My eyes followed him until the door shut behind him and I immediately looked over at Bliss, who was the worst at hiding secrets. It was clear that Gunner wasn't just a guy they were friendly with.

God, why was everything starting to make less sense to me?

Chapter Forty-Six

Harlow

My thoughts were all over the place and I wasn't sure what to think about Jagger ignoring my question about Gunner, and Hunter not even looking at me when he left. I wasn't hurt by the fact that he didn't say goodbye, but more by the hint they both gave me that they were hiding something I couldn't know about. Bliss too. She knew who Gunner was and *just a guy they were friendly with* sounded stupid in my ears, never mind the fact that I still didn't know what Jag and Hunter did when they handled business together.

I promised Jagger never to ask about what he did when he went out. I trusted him not doing anything stupid or illegal, but I knew that was not the case. That one night I had asked Hunter if Jagger ever consumed drugs and his response was simply "who doesn't?" I knew from then on that Jagger wasn't clean, though he hid it from me like a champ. Smoking a joint wasn't that bad in my eyes, and I was sure Jag didn't take any harder drugs. I would've noticed otherwise, right?

Now, all of this drug-thing didn't really bother me. People bought and sold them around Hastings all the time and I had seen people dealing in the middle of the street, not worried about cops seeing them. So why was I taking it so hard to swallow the fact that my brother and the guy I was starting to fall in love with were potential drug dealers?

Potential. That's the word bothering me.

"Where are they going?" I asked Bliss, not minding my own business for once. Hell, I was allowed to ask about where they were going for once.

Bliss's smile didn't meet her eyes and she looked slightly apologetic. "If I knew, I would tell you, darling."

Well, that was a total lie. Straight to my face. But I wasn't going to start a fight with Bliss. She wasn't who I had to get angry with for not telling me. It wasn't her life I worried about.

I nodded slowly, letting it go simply because I didn't want to start any discussion. "Can you at least promise me that they're gonna be safe?" My throat was sore, and talking didn't feel good. Getting air pushed into my lungs through tubes at the hospital really had an effect on my vocal cords and it was the first time I felt like being quiet was okay.

"I can promise you will see them first thing in the morning, if not later tonight." Her eyes were honest and I decided that it was enough for now. I trusted Jagger not to do anything stupid, but

Hunter? Oh my, that man was unpredictable.

"Come on, Low. You must be hungry, and I got some food from Frankie's. He sends you best wishes and an extra slice of chocolate cake. He said you always sneak some bites behind the counter when no one is around," she said with a grin, and I tried not to frown at her anymore. I hadn't even realized I was doing it until my forehead started to ache a little. She was not going to solve any problems which involved Jag and Hunter, so I just had to be patient.

Bliss was nice and sweet. Someone I could call a friend, even if I just met her a few weeks ago. I needed to give her a chance and keep her in my life since I didn't have friends around here. It never really occurred to me that many girls at my college, which I literally never attended anymore, would've been people I could chat with or spend time with. It didn't occur to me because I didn't have the time to go out with people. All my time was used for work at the diner so I could help Jagger financially. I liked it, and since Bliss wasn't a girl from school, I thought she was a good fit for a friend.

"Frankie's cakes are my favorite," I admitted with a smile and walked over to the couch to sit down. Bliss's grin grew wide and she got up from the recliner to get the food she had put in the oven to keep warm. "I love how food brings people together. I mean, the diner I work at is full of football jocks and teenagers who want to feel like they're in one of those cliché, annoying movies. But other than that, I love being a waitress."

I could tell she was excited to spend time with

me. She was all happy, and I started to think that maybe a friend was really all I needed for a long time. I wasn't shy or anything like that, but I just didn't want to open up to people and let them into my life and possibly annoy them with my stories from the past. But Bliss was different in this situation. She knew what she was letting herself into by being my friend, and she seemed to not have any problems with that. Besides that, we both had bad childhood memories. It was funny how it was now Jagger, Bliss, Hunter, and me who came together since we all went through hell as kids.

"Why did you and Hunter get adopted together when you're not related?" Just after asking that I wondered if it was an insensitive question to ask, but Bliss didn't seem to mind at all.

"I guess it was fate. Our parents put us in the orphanage around the same time. Hunter was still a baby and I was three. I remember sitting in a small playroom with Hunter crying in a small hay basket. Almost like a picnic basket. He was wrapped up in a damn towel and I remember wondering if he just had taken a bath. I was too little to understand that his parents didn't really have much to care for him and took the next best things to bring him safely to the orphanage. I sat there with him next to me and listened to him cry until one of the women working at that orphanage, Margie, came in with two duffle bags and a sad smile on her face. I was little, but I remember well what she said to us then. She said that we would be feeling so much better soon and that we would make many new friends to play with. That excited me since I never got to play with other kids. I wanted to make friends and explore, but I also wanted Hunter to stop crying. So I reached for his little hand and looked at him, Margie still standing there watching us. Seconds after touching Hunter's hand he stopped crying, and when he looked at me with those big grey eyes, I simply said, "You don't have to be scared anymore. I will protect you." Margie had told us that story many times while growing up and she said to us that she knew she would only give us up for adoption together. I guess we had a connection that grew stronger each day. I remember running to the other side of the orphanage each day to check on Hunter and play with him." She paused for a second, then let out a small laugh.

"I remember one day we were allowed to play outside in the backyard and I was playing with two other girls. I suddenly heard some boys giggle and say some rude words, so I turned around and saw Hunter crying with a small wound on his face, and about five other boys standing around him with sticks in their hands. I ran up to them and told them to leave him alone or I would do terrible things to them at night. I was seven and Hunter almost four. Those kids were scared of me and ran off. Luckily, Hunter wasn't hurt badly. Just a small cut on the cheek. He was alone most of the time and didn't make friends as easy as I did. Margie also said that he was a little emotionally unstable for his age, always had anger issues, and couldn't sit still for more than ten minutes. We took on the role of taking care of each other and I'm the luckiest to be able to call him my little brother. Even if we don't have that sweet type of sibling relationship you and Jagger have. I love him with all my heart and he knows it. I guess that's all that matters."

CHAPTER FORTY-SEVEN

Harlow

Hunter had issues that came from his early childhood. He couldn't control them and I was starting to put all the pieces together. It made more sense now, knowing the anger he carried around came from way back when he was small. I've always known he had gone through some terrible things to turn out the way he did, and now that Bliss told me more about their past, I understood how a man could possibly switch personalities from one minute to the other. But Bliss hadn't told me everything. Just a little snippet of their lives as kids in the orphanage.

It was sad knowing their parents had left them there at such a young age, but I was glad they found each other. It was hard listening to the words Bliss said, wishing it was Hunter opening up to me like this. Don't get me wrong, I appreciated the fact that Bliss trusted me enough with her story, but Hunter was troubled, and I could tell each time I looked

213

into his eyes there was something dancing around in there that needed to get out. He held back everything, building up hate and rage until he exploded. I got a taste of that before and I couldn't figure out how I would get close to him and help. I wanted to listen to what he had to say. Listen to his own words, describing how he felt.

But for now, I had Bliss's side of the story.

"I'm so sorry, Bliss. But I'm glad you've made it. I mean, you're a strong woman who dealt with all of that and now you're here, still on this earth, and still keeping it up and doing the best you can. You two are lucky to have each other." I smiled, squeezing her hand to let her know I really meant it, even if my voice was weak.

Her sad smile told me she had so much more to say, but I wasn't expecting her to share more with me right now. I wasn't going to push her. "You know, Harlow," she started, now squeezing my hand in return. "We haven't talked much, but Hunter told me many times how special you are. He said the way you use your words to comfort people even if they were in the wrong is like a gift. Most people would use others to talk about their problems, annoy them with their whining, but you, Low, you listen and never judge. You've just confirmed that. And I know Hunter probably never really told you, but he appreciates the way you treat him. He has a troubled mind, sick thoughts most of the time, and I know you calm him down. I'm thankful you're keeping up with him like that."

Her words didn't really make sense. Her sentences were all over the place but I knew where she was going with all of that.

"I'm just trying to get to know him better," I told her. I didn't know what else to say. That's all I've wanted since Hunter and I had that little fight in the kitchen. I had called him an asshole and he got angry, putting his hand on my throat. That's when I realized he wasn't really doing okay.

It was a mental health issue and I knew that topic was a difficult one. I had to take it easy on Hunter.

"You will. Time is all he needs."

I nodded. I could give that to him. Just like he said before at the hospital: "One step at a time."

"Do you and Hunter ever talk? I mean, do you ever have those deep conversations?" I then asked. Bliss puckered up her lips, looking up at the ceiling and then shaking her head.

"We do talk. But we most times just check in on each other. I think that's enough. We're grown-ups. If there's something to say, we say it." She then smiled and tilted her head.

"But you and Jagger," she started. "You two are something else. I've seen siblings being close, but you guys should be getting awards for best brother and sister in the world."

I laughed because I knew there wasn't such a thing as a best brother and sister award. But I see where she was coming from with it. "We had some things happen in our lives which we couldn't really control, and supporting each other was the only thing we had power over. I couldn't imagine life without him. I think I wouldn't have survived without him by my side. He's my superhero."

Bliss smiled again and I could see tears form in

her eyes. "He once told me your parents weren't really there for you," she said, slightly unsure. I nodded. I felt like opening up to her a bit wouldn't hurt either of us. But I wasn't really feeling strong enough to remember my childhood.

"They had other plans than being parents," was all I said, and luckily, it was enough. She nodded, then pointed to the food in front of us. "We should eat. That chocolate cake smells really delicious, and I'm so damn close to eating dessert first."

That made me laugh because the smell of it was bothering me too. I was hungry and junk food soothed me.

We both grabbed a burger and started eating. "Will you spend the night here?" I asked. She shrugged, looking over at the digital clock on the microwave. "I'm not gonna lie. Jagger kind of forced me to stay here until he comes back. He said he doesn't want you here all alone because of Dean."

His name being said won all of my attention. Dean? "I, uh, what?" I didn't understand why Jagger was afraid Dean would show up. All these years he hadn't. So why now?

"Oh, my God," Bliss whispered under her breath and her hand landed on her forehead, telling me she wasn't supposed to tell me that. She looked up at me, her eyes wide. "I'm so stupid."

I frowned. "You're babysitting me." It wasn't a question, more like a fact. "Dean is in town?" I asked then, realizing that it was the only possible reason for Jagger to be worried. Bliss shrugged, then sighed. "I'm not sure. He didn't say Dean's in

Hastings but…" She stopped, looking at me with indecisive eyes.

"But what, Bliss?" I asked, almost frustrated. Why was everybody hiding things from me? Was I this naïve? I was starting to get impatient with everything and everyone. God, how was I the stupid one now?

She sighed again, putting her burger down and looking at her hands. "Jagger told me that Dean called. Again. He's sure Dean's close. Now, I don't know your father, but Jagger said he's an asshole. I'm just here to make sure you're okay. Besides, you just had an accident."

"Right." I didn't have other words. I didn't mean to be angry with Bliss. It wasn't her fault. But finding out Jagger was hiding this thing with Dean bothered the hell out of me.

Chapter Forty-Eight

Harlow

Bliss and I finished eating our food and I didn't really feel like talking. But like I said before, Bliss had nothing to do with what Jagger was hiding from me. I couldn't be mad at her for keeping a secret that wasn't really her business. She was nice enough to keep me company and make sure I was okay since I just came out of the hospital.

It was the very first time I felt some sort of betrayal and anger toward Jagger. I knew I wasn't the type of person to hate or treat others ignorantly just because they did something I didn't approve of, but something in me was telling me that for once in my life, I was allowed to get angry. Angry was a strong word, anyway. I was just a bit confused as to why Jagger wouldn't tell me about Dean being around. If he was scared he might come close to me when he wasn't around, why wouldn't he just stay with me himself?

I watched as Bliss cleaned up the coffee table in

front of me and then brought me a hot cup of tea. She sat back down next to me, sighing and rubbing my back in comfort. "I'm sorry this is all happening."

"It's not your fault, Bliss," I assured her, taking the cup in both my hands and staring down at it. "I just wish Jagger would talk to me more about things like that. I don't care what he does when he's out. I know he has a job at the mechanic's and he earns money the way people should be earning money. He's home when I need him to be. But there's this heavy feeling inside of me that tells me something big is coming my way and I'm not sure I'm ready to take it."

I didn't get an immediate response from her, which only showed me once more that there was something going on I wasn't allowed to know. I looked up to see Bliss stare upfront at the TV. She was blankly staring at it, probably thinking about what she was allowed to say and what she'd rather keep to herself. Perfect.

"It's hard not being part of something that is clearly tearing people apart. I would like to help and I would appreciate it if you could just tell me something about it."

I promised myself not to dig deeper or push her to say anything, yet here I was, being impatient and probably too insistent. I kept my voice low, not wanting to scare her or anything.

"I really shouldn't—" Bliss started to say, but she was interrupted by the front door opening and closing, then heavy footsteps echoed through the hallway behind us.

I turned to see Jagger walk straight to the kitchen, Hunter following close behind while tucking in his gun at the back of his jeans. It wasn't the first time I saw them handling guns or knives, but it was the first time I wondered if they ever pulled the trigger on someone. If they just used those weapons to scare people or to actually hurt them.

Both of them were seemingly irritated and angry. Jagger more so than Hunter. I watched Hunter come to a halt in the living room as he looked at me with dark eyes, then he let out a deep sigh. I was waiting for him to say something when Jagger came back from the kitchen with a beer in his hand. He pointed the bottom of the bottle toward Bliss while looking at Hunter. "Take her home," was all he said before taking long sips from his beer.

"What is happening?" I asked, wondering why I even opened my mouth at this point. Hunter had a gun on him, Jagger was obviously furious, and Bliss had that knowing look on her face that something bad was going on.

"Come on," Hunter said almost in a whisper to his sister and I quickly shot him a glare. How was he ignoring me now? Even before he left, he hadn't said goodbye. Was I the bad guy in this situation or what was going on?

Bliss got up and gave me a small smile before heading toward Hunter. My eyes were back on Jagger, who now leaned against the doorway between the kitchen and living room.

Are they kidding me?

I quickly sat up straight, standing up as fast as I

could. "No. You don't get to just leave without even looking me in the eyes properly," I said to Hunter, frustrated. Then I pointed at my brother, who didn't seem to care for anything right now. "And you…" I let out a laugh that didn't meet the slightest amount of joy in my body. "You need to be honest and truthful with me now."

None of them had expected me to go off like that. Well, it wasn't as dramatic as I thought it was, but it was a start at least. There were secrets in that living room and I was the only one not being part of them. It was starting to bother me so much, that I was seeing a side of me I never even thought existed. And I hated it.

"I don't think this is the time to talk about it," Bliss said, and it was literally the first time since that night I rolled my eyes at Hunter for saying something stupid that I did it again.

"Can you like, not, Bliss?" I asked, surprising myself for being such a bitch.

She slowly nodded and shrugged, then took some steps back behind Hunter and crossed her arms over her chest. I looked at Hunter, then over at Jagger. He took another sip, then tilted his head to the side. He kept his eyes on mine for a while before sighing and shaking his head. "I knew this day would come but I didn't think it would be this soon."

CHAPTER FORTY-NINE

Harlow

Knowing there was something being hidden from me that could change the way I looked at Jagger forever scared me. I realized that he was so much more than just my brother, who I loved deeply, and never in my life was mad at. This time, it was serious. He knew he couldn't keep this from me any longer, and seeing the pain in his eyes hurt me just as much, if not more so.

As for Hunter; there was more to him than what Bliss just told me. He was hurting inside, and keeping it in wasn't going to help much. But it was Hunter we're talking about, and he wouldn't speak his mind. Ever. Maybe pushing him was the best thing to do. I needed to toughen up and tell him that I wanted the truth or he was not going to see me ever again. Of course, that was bullshit. I knew I couldn't go long without seeing him. But this situation with them both hiding something from me made me want to do and say things I never even thought about.

The only thing bothering me was Bliss. She had nothing to do with it and I didn't want her to see how ugly it could get. At least, that's what I imagined the conversation between the guys and me to be. Yet I couldn't just tell her to leave. She was Hunter's sister, and maybe he needed her support in this.

I looked at her, studying her face and trying to find the right words. "I'll leave you three to it," she suddenly said and put her hand on Hunter's shoulder. "I'll call you tomorrow." She kissed his cheek, giving Jagger a quick look and then meeting my gaze with a small smile. "Whatever they tell you, remember that they're doing it for your protection. Especially your brother."

With that, she patted Hunter's shoulder once more and then left. My eyes were already filled with tears, and I wondered how I was going to get through this without having a panic attack. I stared at the door, not wanting to look at them. I could feel their eyes on me, and for once it was making me uncomfortable.

"Come sit down," Jagger said softly, taking a step toward me and reaching out his hand to grab mine. I couldn't believe how my body reacted. I took a few steps back and crossed my arms over my chest carefully. "I think I'll stand."

"You're still hurting, Harlow. Come sit down with us. Please." His voice had a touch of hurt in it and my heart broke right at that moment. I had never intentionally hurt my brother. I never wanted to.

I finally looked up at him, then pulled myself together and went back to sit on the couch. My hands seemed to be the most nervous since they pulled at each other's fingers non-stop. I couldn't help it. I was heating up on the inside and I felt some sort of fear.

I heard footsteps coming toward me and Hunter sat down on the recliner. Almost as if he were keeping some distance between us. But before I could go any further with that thought, Jagger crouched down in front of me and grabbed both my hands in his. He looked up at me with sadness in his eyes. He kept his hands tight around mine, making sure I wasn't running away.

I looked back at him, waiting for him to start this conversation because I wasn't sure how to. He took a deep breath, then he started to speak almost in a whisper. "I need you to promise me one thing, all right? No matter what I say, please don't turn your back on me. I need you. You know you're my whole life and I can't let you run. Can't live without you. Promise me, sweet girl. Promise me you will listen and stay."

He was making it hard on me. How on earth would I ever leave him? He was all I had. But the fact that he was trying to get me to promise him, I knew there were things I wouldn't like. He was being very smart here. We both needed to stick together. I started to nod, then let out a deep sigh. "I promise you."

Something in his eyes lit up and he knew he could trust me with that. Hell, I guess I would even stay with him if he treated me like shit.

"Good. Now promise the same to Hunter."

That was unexpected. To me and Hunter, since he looked at Jagger with a confused look. I gave the same expression back to Hunter, then my brother.

Jagger let out a small laugh. "Listen, he's in this shit with me and he's not getting out of it without me. He still owes me for wanting you, but he's still my best friend. Wouldn't be fair if you would let me get away with it and him not. Now, promise him."

One thing I admired about Jagger was his way of telling his best friend how much he loved him too. And the way he stuck to him and supported him. Jagger had the biggest heart.

I looked over at Hunter, who was probably thinking the same. He was thankful for Jagger. "I promise," I said in a whisper, and Hunter nodded, lifting one corner of his mouth ever so slightly.

My eyes went back to Jagger and I felt his hands squeeze mine. "If you want me to stop talking, just tell me. I figure I have to be as honest as possible, but I don't want you to hear things you couldn't endure."

"I want to hear everything," I told him with determination. He nodded slowly, taking in a deep breath.

"I'll start from the beginning."

CHAPTER FIFTY

Harlow

I watched Jagger closely, waiting for him to speak. He was looking at our hands, his still covering mine and his thumbs caressing the back of my fingers. He was calm but I could tell he was nervous on the inside. This couldn't be easy for him. Or Hunter, who had his elbows propped on his knees now, a cigarette in his hand, and his head low. No matter what would be said tonight, I had to remind myself that I made that stupid promise not to get angry and leave. Stupid, because I wasn't sure there was something in this world they could've done to make me run. I loved Jagger. And Hunter...well, he had a special place in my heart too. I just needed some more time to tell him. I had yet to be sure he felt the same way.

"Please, say something. You're making me more anxious with every second you stay silent," I whispered. The corners of Jagger's mouth lifted slightly, then he looked up at me with sad eyes.

226

"I'm sorry, sweet girl. I'm just trying to figure out how to put my words into real sentences."

I hated seeing him like this. I wasn't the only one in the room feeling all types of negative things and I could tell whatever was coming was hard for him. I had to take it easy on him.

When Jagger still didn't speak, I turned my head to look over at Hunter. He was studying the floor underneath him, picking at his fingernails and letting the cigarette burn down by itself. He had a deep crease between his brows, telling me his thoughts were running wild too. Was I being too hard on them? No, this time I'm allowed to push, I thought.

"I promised you both. I'm here and I won't run. I don't care what it is. I just need you to talk." I felt some tears sting my eyes. All the tension in the room was slowly suffocating me.

"Too damn sweet," Hunter mumbled while shaking his head in what looked like disbelief. I quickly looked back at Jagger, silently pleading for him to explain everything.

He took a deep breath, letting it out slowly before starting to talk. Finally.

"I met Hunter one day at work. His car needed some fixing, and while I worked we started talking. We talked about all sorts of stuff. Guy stuff. And we got to a point where we talked about Dean. I told him about the way he treated us as kids and why I was raising you all alone. I also told him about this shithole we live in. I know I shouldn't put it like that because it's a safe home. The first we've ever had. But you and I both know that this isn't what we

227

deserve. Especially you. But I noticed a long time ago that you don't mind it at all. You're so damn humble. You don't need much to be happy. But back then I wanted more for us." He stopped, taking another deep breath and looking back down at our hands. For now, what he said wasn't scaring me one bit.

I let him collect his thoughts and took a glance at Hunter. He was positioned the same way, elbows on knees, but his eyes were now on mine. I tried to figure out what he was thinking or feeling, but his eyes were dark. When Jagger continued, I looked back at him and braced myself once more.

"Some days later Hunter told me about his job and how he was making good money. Money I could use to fix up this place or even buy a better home. Or money I could use to get us some more food. Better food. I was interested in all of that. I quickly started to imagine a better life for us and the best thing was, it was quick money. You do the job, you get the cash. So I told him I was in."

I was waiting for something big to be said. Something to knock me off my feet. But the way he told this story was making it mysterious. The tension rose from sentence to sentence and I was ready to hear how it ended.

"Just tell me what you do, please," I begged. I needed this to be over so I could forgive them and move on with my life.

Jagger looked over at Hunter and they exchanged looks I wasn't sure I understood. It was almost as if Hunter was telling Jagger to relax or to take a step back. But I could've been wrong about either.

Jagger's eyes were back on mine.

"I'll make this quick," he said. "We sell drugs, guns, and ammunition." He was quiet after that and I watched his face closely. I wasn't sure if there was more, but I kept quiet just to make sure not to interrupt him. When he didn't speak, I started to wonder if he was telling the whole truth. I knew there were drug dealers around town and I suspected them of dealing too. Hearing him confirm it didn't really do it for me.

"Do you do drugs?" I asked, hoping I didn't regret that question later on.

"Not the ones that could kill me," he said. "Weed, that's all."

"What about your black eyes and bloody noses, then?" I knew he did underground fighting. I wasn't stupid. I found out a long time ago and I wasn't even sure anymore if he told me once or if I had just known for so long that I didn't remember us having a conversation about it.

"Dealing isn't just two people meeting and exchanging money and drugs with a friendly atmosphere, Harlow." Yeah, no shit, Sherlock.

"Have you ever used that gun?" I then asked, looking over at Hunter and nodding toward his waist. "And you?" I added.

Both of them nodded once, and somehow it seemed to be good enough of an answer for me.

I looked back at Jagger, wondering why he made such a big deal out of this and making me promise not to run off. There was more to this. And I knew he would've told me if Hunter hadn't silently stopped him. There was one thing that interested me

more than the drugs and guns.
    "So, where is all that money?"

CHAPTER FIFTY-ONE

Harlow

Jagger kept quiet after my question. He looked unsure and I could tell he was debating whether or not to tell me about it.

"You said you make good money. So, where is it? What did you do with it?" I didn't care about the way I sounded. I had an icy tone in my words and I surprised myself with the way I talked to my brother. But this was serious. He just told me about his job, knowing it probably wasn't the whole truth, but I wasn't challenging him to spill all his secrets. If he needed some more time to tell me about it, I would give it to him. This was a good start. A bit late to tell me, but it was enough for now.

Instead of answering me, Jagger stood back up, letting go of my hands. I watched as he walked over to the bathroom, and for a second I wasn't sure if I should follow him or not. I looked over at Hunter, who gave me a nod in Jagger's direction. He was silently telling me to follow my brother and see what he was going to do. I got up, making sure my body was steady enough, and walked up behind Jagger, who was now standing in the bathroom in front of the toilet. Confused, I eyed the tiny white-tiled room, then watched as Jagger bent down next to the toilet. He reached for the wall with both hands, easily taking off a big tile and revealing a little hole. I was still unsure of what was going on and I hoped he soon would explain to me why there was a hidden hole in our bathroom wall. Jagger got back up and turned to look at me. His glance behind me let me know that Hunter was standing in the doorway right at my back and I realized I had no way to get out of here. It was almost as if they wanted to make sure I really wouldn't run.

I kept my eyes on Jagger, waiting for him to explain whatever was going on. Then he held out his hand, revealing a card which he held between his fore and middle finger. I looked down at it, noticing it was a credit card.

"Everything I ever earned is saved in this bank account. I don't remember how much money there is in there right now, but I stopped checking the numbers after a hundred thousand."

My body went numb. I stared at the card with Jagger's name on it and my thoughts were, once again, all over the place.

"When did you stop counting?" I asked, still in disbelief. Jagger shrugged, pushing his fists into his pockets. "Don't know. About three years ago."

I let out a harsh laugh and rested my hands on my hips. My eyes shot up to Jagger's and a humorless laugh escaped my chest. "Are you fucking kidding me?"

Not sure why, but I was furious. Money never was something I cared greatly about. I grew up with a little amount, made it through middle school with even less, and now I was happy I had enough to get some food each day. And he was only just now telling me, that he had more money in that stupid bank account than I could've ever imagined?

"Let me explain, Low." Jagger was calm and his eyes were full of regret. "I know it's not fair to hide this from you, but I was going to tell you sooner or later. It's just…" he sighed, shaking his head. "We don't need it. I don't need it. And we both know we could easily go on with our lives without having full wallets."

"Then why do you have this?" I asked, holding up the credit card and shoving it against his chest. He took it from me, letting out another deep sigh. "Because as soon as you finish college I want you to have it all. God, that sounds so damn stupid." He took a deep breath, letting his head fall.

I watched him closely, hearing my thoughts telling me that he was right and that I didn't need any money to be happy. But it just didn't make sense. At all.

"His point is," Hunter started to say and I quickly turned around to look at him. His eyes were instantly on mine and I couldn't help but relax a little at the sight in front of me. He was leaning against the doorway, both his hands in his front pockets and a new cigarette tucked behind his left ear. Damn him.

"He's looking out for a better future. He wants

you to finish college, even though it's a shit school. And he doesn't want you to change anything in your life right now. He sees how humble you are. How grateful, even though you don't get to spend any of the money you earn at the diner on yourself. You never complain about not having the newest clothes or having a perfectly furnished bedroom. You accept all of this even though it's a shithole. You care about others much more than you do about yourself and that, my love, that's your biggest gift. Your brother talks about you exactly the way I just did almost every week. We see who you truly are."

His words affected me in a way that made my body feel warm and protected. Yet I didn't quite understand what Jagger's goal with it all was. I slowly turned back around to look at Jagger. "He pretty much said it all. But that still doesn't explain why I keep that much money hidden from you when we could've used it to buy a bigger house or a better car." He reached out to me, and I took the two steps between us to stand directly in front of him. He grabbed my face with both his hands, wiping away the tears on my cheek. "This city isn't safe and I can't quit my job just like that. We had to sign a contract."

"With Gunner," I said. They talked about him once before and they were all very secretive about him. So why not assume that he was the famous drug lord in Hastings?

Jagger pressed his lips into a thin line, then nodded. "Yes, Gunner. My contract with him doesn't end until next summer. That's when you will be done with college. That was my plan. As soon as you're done, we'll leave Hastings and start all over. That is if that's what you want. But for now, we have to stay. And spending money in this city will probably cause a stir."

I studied his face for a while, wondering if what he was saying made any sense. It somehow did. And I thought I could let him get away with that for now.

CHAPTER FIFTY-TWO

Harlow

I watched Jagger studying my face while still holding my head firmly between his hands. I replayed all the things he said to me in my head just to make sure I didn't miss anything important. I couldn't find anything that made me want to ask more about all of this. It all started to make sense. And I realized he was doing it all for me. Risking his life just to make sure my future would be better than now. He was looking out for me, just like he did when we were little.

"Please, say something," Jagger whispered with a sad smile. My heart felt full, even if what he did was illegal, and he still was carrying a gun and drugs on him daily. And I knew, no matter what Jagger did to keep me safe and alive, I would be thankful.

I put my arms around his waist, leaning my body and head against him and closing my eyes tightly. He returned my hug carefully, making sure not to hurt me. His hand cupped the back of my head and I could feel him relax. "I just need you to be careful."

"I am. I promise you that."

That was enough for now. I wasn't sure how long we stood there like that, but when we let go of each other and I turned to look at Hunter, he was gone and the front door shut. I looked at Jagger with a questioning look.

"He probably had something to take care of. Come on, it's late."

We walked out of the bathroom and Jagger immediately steered me toward my bedroom. "You need some rest. Tomorrow's a new day and we can have a talk then if you want to."

I looked at him and gave him a nod. "Okay. Good night, Jag." He took a step toward me, kissing my forehead the way he always did. "Good night, Low."

I never really had nightmares, but this time, I had to watch as some masked guys shot my brother right in front of my eyes. It was horrible, and luckily, the dream ended quickly. I woke up early in the morning, darkness still filling my room thanks to the heavy rain falling. The typical Hastings weather was kinda comforting this morning, almost as if it was washing away all the bad things that happened in the last few weeks.

I decided to take a shower and get dressed, then make breakfast. It was almost seven-thirty, and waking up this early without an alarm felt good. Sleeping in was never really my thing.

Showered and ready for the day, I started to cook some eggs and bacon, knowing the smell of it would wake up Jagger. The few times I got to make breakfast at home were my favorite mornings. Working at the diner never really gave me the chance to cook breakfast at home and make sure Jagger would eat before leaving the house.

As I took the bacon out of the pan, footsteps came my direction and I turned to see Jagger coming through the kitchen door with messy hair and tired eyes. "Morning," I said with a smile, then put a plate with eggs and bacon on the table.

"Sleep well?" was his response and I nodded.

"You?" I asked, then put another plate on the table and turned off the stove.

"Yeah, missed waking up to this." I bet.

We ate breakfast and he asked me more than once if I had any questions about the things we talked about yesterday. I didn't want to bring up any of it. I was okay with the way things were at the moment. So I changed the subject.

"Could you do me a favor, Jagger?" I asked, taking the last sip of my coffee. He nodded, leaning back and crossing his hands behind his head.

"Could you give me a ride to Hunter's?" I wasn't sure if that was the best idea, but I needed to clear some things up with him. The situation we were in was weird and I needed some clarification.

Jagger took his time answering me. "If he's okay with it, sure."

I could tell that he still wasn't so sure about me spending time with Hunter. But I guess he couldn't really do much about it when I was the one wanting to see Hunter.

"I will text him and ask."

Jagger nodded and got up, taking the plates and cups from the table and putting them into the sink. "I'll take a shower. I have to be at work by ten, so I could drop you off if he's okay with it." With work, he meant the mechanic's. Why would he sell drugs during the day when literally anyone could see him, right?

I had a hard time figuring out what to text Hunter, so I stared at his number for a while before calling him. I thought talking was much easier than texting. At the fifth ring, he picked up, and when he talked I realized it probably was still too early for him. "Good morning, love," he said, his voice raspy and low. Damn him, once again.

His words made me smile. "Good morning," I said, sitting down on the couch. "I didn't mean to wake you, I'm sorry."

"It's okay. I was about to get up, anyway."

"Oh, so, are you up to something today?" I asked, hoping he wasn't.

"Not really."

"Okay."

Oh. Good. Now what? He didn't really sound interested in doing anything. God, I was bad at this.

"Was there something you wanted to say?" he asked, his voice amused, and I realized that I wasn't talking for a little too long.

"Yeah," I said, sighing. Why was I nervous all of a sudden? "I was just wondering if I could come by your place."

"My place?" he asked and I immediately regretted my offer.

"Yeah, but…" I sighed again, shaking my head.

"I'm sorry. That's a stupid idea. I know you don't want that. Why did I even ask." I whispered the last part and I was ready to hang up on him.

"I'd love to have you here."

"What?"

He chuckled. "I said, I would love to have you here with me." Oh, okay. That's good.

"Okay, great. I mean, thank you." And with that, I covered my face with my hand, embarrassed by myself.

"You're too fucking adorable, love. I'll be home. Just come by whenever. Can't wait to see you again."

He hung up after that and I hated myself for being such an idiot. It was Hunter's fault I couldn't think straight ninety-nine percent of the time. After all, no matter what was going on in his life and no matter how much wrong he did in the past, I would stick to him. The same applied to Jagger. The more I found out about their lives, the more I wanted them close. I had this strange feeling inside of me that something big was coming my way. More secrets being exposed and more things I would have to handle and accept. No matter how much damage it would bring, I knew I would stay strong and figure out a way to adjust to it. In the end, that's what I've been doing all my life. That's what I was good at. No matter how much someone hurt me in the past, I would always forgive.

Acknowledgements

When I first started writing at thirteen, I never thought about sending one of my manuscripts to publishers, or even letting anyone read them. Writing was something I wanted to keep to myself. My safe place to calm down. But with this story, I wanted others to read it.

Writing this book didn't take long and it felt good sending it off to see if someone would give it a chance. Luckily, Limitless Publishing did just that and I can't describe how thankful I am for this opportunity.

Thanks to everyone at Limitless Publishing who helped create this book from cover design to editing and a special thanks to Toni who made this very first experience with an editor fun and helpful.

A big thank you to Katy Bucher who is one of my best friends. Because of you I keep my imagination running wild and you literally inspired me to write this story with one idea you had.

And finally: to my mom. You are the biggest part of my life and you showed me how strong a woman can be even after years of struggling.

About The Author

Vanessa Siena is a twenty-something-year-old student with Italian roots living in Switzerland, where she was born and raised. Spending most of her free time as a teenager writing, she one day decided to upload her first official work "HUNTER" on Wattpad, where she reached over 100'000 reads in less than five months. When she's not writing, she plays bass guitar, reads novels and likes to eat to pass the time. Being very inspired by the '80s, rock bands from that time are always playing in the background.

Social Media Links

Instagram:
https://www.instagram.com/authorvanessasiena/

Wattpad:
https://www.wattpad.com/user/harlovv

Join our Reader Group on Facebook and don't miss out on meeting our authors and entering epic giveaways!

Limitless Reading

Where reading a book
is your first step to becoming
limitless...

LIMITLESS PUBLISHING *Reader Group*

Join today! *"Where reading a book is your first step to becoming limitless..."*

https://www.facebook.com/groups/Limitless Reading/